ADVANCE PRAISE

"Haunting in its implications, astute in its observations about how polarized we've become around the simple question of what it means to be human, Daniel Olivas's *Chicano Frankenstein* is ultimately an empathetic exploration of the heart told in spare, but beautiful prose. Olivas is a master storyteller and this book is another of his triumphs!"

—Rubén Degollado,
author of *The Family Izquierdo*

"In a near-future Pasadena, Daniel A. Olivas resurrects Mary Shelley's creation to glorious effect, making it clear who the monsters really are in a world where a cynical government sees resurrected humans as pawns to use, abuse, and discard. The real trick of this speculative political satire is that corruption and peril coexist with compassion, humor, and large doses of Chicano joy. I loved every page-turning minute!"

—Michelle Ruiz Keil,
author of *Summer in the City of Roses*

"In Daniel A. Olivas's alt-world political satire *Chicano Frankenstein*, we follow his reanimated main character, 'the man,' in his search for identity in a world that is increasingly hostile to him and his kind. With its tongue firmly planted in its cheek, this important novel is at once frightening and humorous, and I found myself laughing out loud more than once as Olivas cleverly delivered his cautionary message, served with a basket of fresh baked pan dulce."

—Orlando Ortega-Medina,
author of *The Fitful Sleep of Immigrants*

"In the genre-bending tradition of Mary Shelley, Daniel A. Olivas's latest novel *Chicano Frankenstein* expertly stitches together gothic political satire, science fiction, and existential metafiction to expose the racist and classist hypocrisies that undergird the American political economy under tyrannical right-wing leaders."

—Eileen M. Hunt,
author of *Artificial Life After Frankenstein*

"If you're looking for a reverberating literary experiment in a speedy read, Daniel A. Olivas's *Chicano Frankenstein* is the book for you. In this literary pastiche of timeless novels, beloved TV, and familiar political narratives, the love story of Faustina and the man will reanimate your deepest expectations of humanism into new understandings of monstrosity."

—Xochitl Gonzalez,
author of *Olga Dies Dreaming*

PAST PRAISE

"… a major American talent."
—Luis Alberto Urrea, author of *Good Night, Irene*

"Olivas is adept at establishing character in a sentence or two; he creates an image, a moment of self-deception, in which we come to know these characters intimately and easily imagine their entire lives …"

—*Los Angeles Times*

"An important voice in Latinx literature."

—*BuzzFeed*

"Olivas is a literary marvel."

—*Shelf Awareness*

CHICANO FRANKENSTEIN

DANIEL A. OLIVAS

FOREST AVENUE PRESS
Portland, Oregon

Library of Congress Cataloging-in-Publication Data

Names: Olivas, Daniel A., author.
Title: Chicano Frankenstein / Daniel A. Olivas.
Description: Portland, Oregon: Forest Avenue Press, 2024. | Summary: "An unnamed paralegal, brought back to life through a controversial process, maneuvers through a near-future world that both needs and resents him. As the United States president spouts anti-reanimation rhetoric and giant pharmaceutical companies rake in profits, the man falls in love with lawyer Faustina Godínez. His world expands as he meets her network of family and friends, setting him on a course to discover his first-life history, which the reanimation process erased. With elements of science fiction, horror, political satire, and romance, Chicano Frankenstein confronts our nation's bigotries and the question of what it truly means to be human."--Provided by publisher.
Identifiers: LCCN 2023034805 | ISBN 9781942436591 (paperback) | ISBN 9781942436607 (epub)
Subjects: LCGFT: Science fiction. | Novels.
Classification: LCC PS3615.L58 C55 2024 | DDC 813/.6--dc23/eng/20240731
LC record available at https://lccn.loc.gov/2023034805

Forest Avenue Press LLC
P.O. Box 80134
Portland, OR 97280
forestavenuepress.com

Printed in the United States

Distributed by Publishers Group West

1 2 3 4 5 6 7 8 9

For my father,
Michael Augustine Olivas (1932–2020)

And for my brother,
David J. Olivas (1960–2023)

CHICANO FRANKENSTEIN

Daniel A. Olivas

Forest Avenue Press
Portland, Oregon

"I am malicious because I am miserable.
Am I not shunned and hated by all mankind?"
—Mary Wollstonecraft Shelley, *Frankenstein*

"One time he stopped at mid-turn and fear suddenly set in.
He realized that he had called himself.
And thus the lost year began."
—Tomás Rivera, ... *y no se lo tragó la tierra* /
... *And the Earth Did Not Devour Him*

PRES. CADWALLADER PROMISES TO SIGN "ANTI-STITCHER" LAW

CAMP DAVID, MD (AP)—Speaking to reporters on Saturday, President Mary Beth Cadwallader pledged to sign a landmark anti-reanimation bill into law on Tuesday after the House and Senate passed it last week. The president said that it would deliver the "final plank" of her ambitious domestic agenda as she aims to boost her party's standing with voters about three months before the midterm elections.

The legislation—dubbed the anti-stitcher law by its supporters—would ban the medical technology known as reanimation that had been pioneered by German scientists a decade ago. The technology made possible what had only been imagined in folklore and horror novels: the reanimation of once-dead human tissue eventually resulting in over 12 million documented cases of human reanimation subjects in the U.S. alone. The worldwide number is uncertain, though the World Health Organization estimated that there may be more than 100 million reanimated subjects living across the globe.

Due to the recently perfected technology permitting the joining of body parts from multiple cadavers to complete a whole person, the resulting reanimated subjects became commonly known by the crude epithet "stitchers" in a reference to the joining of various body parts that requires, in part, the suturing together of flesh and muscle.

The legislation has strong backing from the country's religious leaders who had decried animation as playing God. However, organized labor as well as the national and numerous local chambers of commerce lobbied the White House to veto the bill asserting that the reanimation technology benefited the sagging economy by supplying a potentially inexhaustible new source of young, healthy workers.

"This technology can't be used to reanimate the elderly or infirmed," observed Carlos Moraga, president of the U.S. Chamber of Commerce. "But it works like a dream to bring back otherwise healthy workers at all levels of the economy, which is good for America. And if we pull the plug on the reanimation industry, we'll be behind the eight ball with other countries that are going full steam ahead with replenishing their workforce through reanimation."

Anti-immigrant groups were divided on the issue because the creation of a reanimated population could eventually diminish employers' reliance on and hunger for low-wage foreign workers. However, those same groups complained that "stitchers" were not "real Americans" and could replace native-born U.S. residents in the near future if reanimation ramped up.

In anticipating a triumphant signing ceremony at the White House, Cadwallader pointed to the bill as proof that democracy—no matter how long or untidy the process—can still deliver for American voters. The president road-tested a line she will likely repeat later this fall ahead of the midterm elections: "Real Americans and human decency won, and the special interests lost."

Chapter One

THE MAN SAT ALONE at his kitchen island. Today he needed to go into the office, but for now, he wore a white T-shirt, boxers, and slippers. The man looked down at two slices of buttered wheat toast that sat on a plate near a steaming mug of coffee. He breathed in the aroma of his breakfast and attempted to affix a word to what he felt at that moment. The bright morning sun shone through the kitchen window onto his breakfast and illuminated it like a stage where the actors stood frozen before uttering their opening lines. The man considered his breakfast.

What do I feel?

That was the question he often asked himself. The man knew he should feel something as he looked upon his daily morning meal, a meal that never changed, at least not in recent times.

What do I feel?

The man sensed something watching him. He turned his head toward the kitchen window and squinted. *Ah!* The neighbor's cat, Nacho, sat at the far end of his apartment complex's communal backyard on the low retaining wall and stared at him. Not a threat. Just a tiger-striped feline. Nacho blinked, licked its lips, and scurried away. The man turned back to his breakfast and placed both hands, palms down, on either side of his plate. The cool white quartz felt solid, secure on his skin.

Is that what I feel? Solid, secure?

The man then focused on the contours of his hands. His left hand was a full two inches longer and an inch wider than his right. And his right hand was much darker than his left. He did feel something.

I feel remorse.

Remorse that his hands were such a mismatch that people often stared and children pointed. Even when he tried to hide the vast differences between his hands by wearing gloves in the winter, people noticed—especially children, whose line of vision brought them eye-to-eye, as it were, with his mismatched appendages.

What do I feel?

Hungry. And so now this breakfast of buttered wheat toast and hot coffee served a purpose. He reached for one piece of toast and brought it to his lips. He held it there for a moment and attempted to confirm that he was indeed hungry.

Yes. I feel hungry.

The man bit into the toast and chewed.

"Is there any of that for me, guapo?"

The man turned and watched the woman walk behind the island, open one cabinet and then another until she found a coffee mug, and pour herself a cup. She turned toward the man.

"Any half-and-half left?"

Before the man could respond, the woman opened the refrigerator, scanned its contents, and emitted a pleased *yes!* before retrieving a small carton of half-and-half. After the woman lightened her coffee to the appropriate shade of brown, she returned the carton to the refrigerator, walked around the edge of the island, and plopped down on the stool next to the man.

"I hope you don't mind that I used your very manly-man deodorant, guapo."

"I don't mind," said the man.

"I just wish you had a hair dryer."

The man noticed the woman's thick, curly, black hair bounce and set free water droplets that lightly sprinkled the kitchen island and her black pantsuit. The woman smelled like the man's shampoo mixed with the pungent scent of his Irish Spring deodorant. He liked how she smelled—his Irish Spring took on a subtler scent on her—and appreciated the woman's glistening hair. The man thought about the woman's wish that he had a hair dryer.

"Toast?" said the woman.

"Yes," said the man.

"That's your breakfast?"

"Yes."

"Do you have something a little more Mexican?"

"Like what?"

"Pan dulce?"

"No, I don't."

"How about a cheese blintz? I'm happy to honor my Jewish stepfather."

"No, I don't have that either."

The woman reached over and snatched the untouched piece of toast.

"Ni modo," said the woman. "I have to watch my carbs. Healthful wheat toast it is for me."

They sat in silence as they both crunched on their toast.

After three minutes, she said, "You know, guapo, this is the second time I've stayed over."

"Yes, it is."

"And this is the second time I've wondered if you've had something other than toast for breakfast."

"Yes, it is."

"And I know you've got a thoughtful side to you."

"I do."

The woman chuckled at the concise man's response. In three quick bites, she finished eating the piece of toast and washed it down with a loud gulp of coffee.

"But you do make good coffee, guapo. That, I admit."

"Thank you," said the man. A small smile crept onto his freshly shaven face.

The woman stood, put her coffee mug into the sink, walked back to the man, pecked him on his left cheek.

"I'll bring the pan dulce or maybe blintzes next time," she said. "If there is a next time."

"Thank you," said the man. "I hope there is a next time."

"Oh, you sweet talker," said the woman. "Maybe I'll bring both."

"Thank you."

"Need to grab my purse," said the woman. "I've got young lawyers and law clerks to boss around, a law practice to run, corporations to sue, judges to cajole. Are you going to work today too?"

"Yes," said the man. "After."

"After what?"

The man thought. "After I go for a run and then make a trip to the pharmacy."

"Got it," said the woman. "Life's errands and exercise wait for no one."

"I usually run at night. "

"Well, I guess I ruined your routine last night."

The man listened as the woman walked away from him to retrieve her purse from the man's bedroom. The man wondered if the woman was examining his bedroom, and if so, what she thought of it in the light of day. The woman returned after a few moments and stood near the man.

"Hasta luego, my laconic hookup," said the woman.

"Goodbye," said the man.

The man stared at his cup of coffee as the woman stood near him. They remained in silence for several seconds listening to each other breathe. The woman eventually turned and walked to the front door. The man stared at his cup of coffee as he listened to the woman clear her throat. After a few seconds more, the woman opened the door and left. The man could discern the woman's heels click down the walkway toward her car. The woman's Irish Spring–infused scent lingered. The man nodded and acknowledged what he had observed before: his soap smelled different on her. He appreciated the difference and wondered what the science was behind it, if indeed there was a scientific explanation for it. Perhaps it was all his imagination, nothing more.

The man took another bite of his toast as the woman's car started up with a *vroom*.

The man chewed his toast and then took another bite as he thought.

What is her name?

The man concentrated.

Her name...

The man closed his eyes for three seconds, and then his eyes popped open.

Ah! Faustina.

The man felt something, and though he was not yet certain what it was, he knew what he felt was something definable, something provoked by the fact that, if he concentrated, he could retrieve essential information when needed.

The man thought for a moment.

What do I feel?

The man smiled. He finally recognized this feeling, though he did not experience it often. But he knew that he felt it at that moment.

Pride.

The man smiled and emitted a small chuckle. But then his feeling of pride gave way to something else. Something entirely different. The man concentrated again, searching for the right word to describe what he now felt. What was it?

Shame.

The man's face grew hot. Perspiration covered his upper lip and forehead.

Shame.

The man should have remembered Faustina's name easily, without effort, because he had said it many times last night in bed as well as on the previous Friday, their first night together. He liked the feel of her name on his tongue. *Faustina.* They'd met at the annual environmental law conference in Yosemite. The partners at his law firm usually didn't let the paralegals attend, but they'd had a particularly good year, with three large settlements coming in during the spring and summer. So the partners felt generous enough to hold a lottery to see which of the firm's five paralegals could go along with the firm's attorneys to the annual conference. The man won the lottery by choosing the lowest number scrawled on a small brown slip of paper pulled out of a Dodgers cap. His fellow paralegals were collectively rather annoyed since the man was junior to them all. The man did not feel any remorse for being victorious because he had won purely by chance. But now the man experienced a wave of shame because he had not immediately remembered Faustina's name. And it should have been easy. She was a partner in a boutique firm, and the firm's name imprinted itself on his memory because he had read Faustina's business card many times over the last week: GODÍNEZ, TSUKAMAKI & STONE. But his eyes never seemed to move beyond the large letters of the firm's name emblazoned on the business card, otherwise Faustina's name would have come to him easily. The man believed that he had a very visual memory. He concentrated. Which surname was hers? Think… think… think… *Ah!* He remembered that Faustina was the founding partner of the firm, so her surname would be first.

Faustina Godínez.

The man said the woman's name aloud.

Faustina Godínez.

The man would never forget her name, unless he wanted to.

Faustina Godínez.

The man's shame vanished almost as fast as it had emerged. He smiled. After a few moments, he sensed that he was being watched again. The man turned toward the window and squinted. But Nacho was nowhere to be seen. The man let out a small, almost indecipherable laugh as he returned to his breakfast of buttered toast and coffee.

And then it happened, as it often did, without warning: his mind flashed to images from his recurring nightmare from last night. The man shivered, closed his eyes, shook his head to cast out the images. He opened his eyes. What did the dream mean? Why did it come to him night after night after night? It was as if some unseen malicious power played cruel games with him. But to what purpose? What did the man ever do to anyone? But this was pure fantasy. There was no unseen power playing tricks on him. Dreams were not real. They came in different flavors, just like candy or ice cream or poison. There were daydreams, false-awaking dreams, lucid dreams, nightmares, prophetic dreams, epic dreams, mutual dreams, and many more. Perhaps the brain just working things out. Who knows? He read someplace that dreams don't actually mean anything at all. They are only made up of electrical brain impulses that pull random thoughts and imagery from our memories. But if this was true, what memories fueled the man's recurring nightmare? What were the building blocks for this bizarre dreamscape that invaded his nightly slumber? He had no memory of incidents that could fuel this nightmare, no experiences that would have been the foundation for what he experienced each night while he slumbered.

After a few moments, the man sensed that he was being watched again. He turned toward the window and squinted. And there sat Nacho on the retaining wall, staring directly at the man. He waved to the cat, but it did not move. The man wondered what Nacho thought. Did the man become fodder for Nacho's dreams? Was the man nothing but a cipher to the cat, something to be studied and observed from afar and with a relentless feline gaze? Or perhaps Nacho didn't even notice the man but stared at something else in the house that looked so much more interesting. Perhaps a tasty treat? And then the man wondered if cats even had thoughts. How can you have thoughts without words? Maybe cats were a bundle of instincts, nothing more. But perhaps meows were words, to cats at least. Meows—and don't forget purrs and hisses—were forms of communication, weren't they? The man turned back to his coffee and drank. It was cold. Breakfast was done. Time to move on.

Chapter Two

FAUSTINA GODÍNEZ ENTERED THE conference room carrying a file and notepad under her right arm and holding a white coffee mug in her left hand. The mug had the word *CHINGONA* emblazoned across it in large yellow letters. She settled into one of the leather chairs and arranged her file, notepad, and coffee mug before her. The law firm's other name partners sat across from each other and continued to discuss a summary judgment hearing that Grace Tsukamaki had just covered for one of the senior associates who had come down with a horrid flu. Leonard Stone nodded and chuckled as Grace imitated the somewhat cranky judge who had presided over the hearing. Faustina suddenly realized that a large platter of pan dulce sat in the middle of the conference table. She couldn't believe her luck. *Ask and ye shall receive!* Faustina stood and reached over toward the platter, eyeing a pink concha. Without pausing her monologue, Grace leaned forward and gently slapped Faustina's hand away from the platter.

"I made a special trip to La Monarca just to get those!" said

Grace in an exaggerated motherly tone despite her being seven years younger than Faustina. "They're for the team meeting in less than an hour. We need to keep our young lawyers and paralegals happy and hyped up on sugar."

"But…" pleaded Faustina.

"And I don't want anyone ruining the pan dulce's perfect symmetry, not even the firm's senior partner," added Grace. "I stacked them just so. You can wait, can't you?"

Faustina complied and fell back into her chair. She would never tolerate such scolding from anyone but Grace for some reason. Leonard chuckled at his two partners. His phone suddenly beeped.

"Oh, shit," said Leonard as he studied a new text.

"What's up?" said Faustina.

"The jury came back with a question."

"But they just started deliberating yesterday afternoon," said Grace. "What do you think it means?"

"It means," said Leonard as he gathered up a file and stood, "I need to run to court and meet Sahar so we can get back to the courtroom and let the judge tell us what's up."

"I hope it's a question like 'May we give plaintiffs every single thing their brilliant trial counsel asked for?'" said Faustina.

"I am sure that's exactly what the jury is asking," chuckled Leonard. "But toxic torts can have some tough questions of causation. It's probably nothing, just jury confusion with the instructions which, I admit, were a bit more complicated than I would have liked."

"Let us know as soon as you can!" said Grace.

Leonard looked down at the platter of pan dulce and paused.

"Okay, you may take a piece," said Grace.

Faustina frowned.

"And take a piece for Sahar too," added Grace. She plucked

two paper napkins from a plastic package and slid them toward Leonard. "You two need your energy."

"You are too kind," said Leonard as he grabbed the napkins and two pieces of pan dulce. "We will remain happy warriors." With that, Leonard left.

"Really?" said Faustina.

"What?"

"Leonard and Sahar outrank me?"

"No, absolutely not," said Grace. "That was an exception to the rule based upon a litigation emergency."

"Oh, that's clear."

"And besides, by taking two pieces," said Grace as she rearranged the remaining pieces of pan dulce, "I was able to maintain the symmetry of the whole presentation."

"Oh, so now you're applying principles of feng shui to pan dulce?"

"Don't be racist," said Grace, feigning indignation. "I'm Japanese, not Chinese."

"It's a universal concept," said Faustina.

"You don't even know what feng shui really means."

Faustina reached for her phone and looked down at her lap. After a few seconds, she said: "The five elements of feng shui—earth, metal, water, wood, and fire—come from the Taoist tradition. The elements are five interrelated phases in life that work together to create a complete system. Typically, when you feng shui your home, you balance these five elements."

"Are you reading from Wikipedia?" said Grace.

Faustina grinned, lifted her phone from her lap, and showed the screen to Grace.

"You can learn many fascinating things from this little gizmo," said Faustina.

"Okay, enough of this silliness," said Grace. "Now to

more important things before the troops show up for our weekly meeting."

"What's more important than principles of feng shui?" said Faustina. She put her phone down on the conference table.

"Tell me about the handsome paralegal from the Yosemite conference."

Faustina looked away.

"Well?" said Grace.

"Well what?" said Faustina before sipping her coffee.

"Is he your first Irish Spring man?"

Faustina almost spat out her coffee as she muffled a laugh.

"I mean, come on," continued Grace, "I can smell your new scent all the way over here."

Faustina struggled to regain her composure and swallow the last bit of coffee.

"And your hair is so curly right now, it's clear you did not have the benefit of a hair dryer this morning."

"Stop it!" said Faustina.

"And while I love that suit and blouse, I think a change of clothes would have helped you keep your little sleepover a secret from me, your very best friend in the whole goddamned world."

"Okay, okay," said Faustina in surrender. "Yes, that nice paralegal and I have spent some quality time together."

"I knew it!"

"But it's a casual thing."

"So what," said Grace, leaning in. "Things were casual with me and Brandon until…"

"Until?"

"Until they weren't."

"This is nothing like you and Brandon."

"And now, four years of marriage and one toddler later, it should be quite clear to you that a very 'casual thing,'" continued

Grace as she added air quotes for emphasis, "can morph into a very un-casual thing before you know it."

"Thank you, counselor," said Faustina. "I will take your argument under submission."

"I'm just saying…"

"I know what you're saying, my friend."

"I want to be in on the ground floor," said Grace, "because I am your oldest and wisest friend who can give you the best advice that money can buy."

"Oh, so now you're charging?"

"Day care is expensive," said Grace. "And you know Brandon is a high school teacher. He has a heart of gold and a bank account to match his giving nature."

"Tell you what," said Faustina.

"What?"

"After work, let's grab a drink and I will spill my guts."

"Yes!"

"But, of course, you might be buying the first round."

"Not a problem!" said Grace as she started texting.

"What are you doing?"

"I am letting my handsome life partner know that I will be a bit late tonight because my beautiful law partner needs to spill her soul out to me over many, many drinks."

"You are a very responsible and conscientious life partner. I hope Brandon doesn't mind."

"No," said Grace as she put down her phone. "He has a little crush on you anyway."

"Stop it!"

"It's true!"

"No it's not."

"And I don't mind," said Grace. "It means he has good taste."

Faustina sighed.

"And we have an agreement that if I should die young and you're still single or in a rocky marriage that needs ending, he may court you without any guilt whatsoever."

"Oh, thank you," said Faustina. "I always wanted to be someone's sloppy seconds."

"You could do worse!"

"So true," said Faustina. "So true."

"I am so excited for you!"

"Don't get too excited, my friend."

"And if this works out with Mr. Irish Spring," said Grace, "all three partners of this lovely boutique firm will have found their handsome, loving husbands."

"Ay," said Faustina as she buried her face into her palms.

"Can you imagine triple-dating with me, Leonard, and our hunky husbands? Finally, a perfect balance!"

"Yes, I agree," surrendered Faustina, "three couples would be better balanced than two couples and an oddball."

"And that's what I would call 'feng shui,'" said Grace.

"But you're not Chinese."

"A brilliant woman once told me that feng shui is a universal concept."

A group of attorneys and paralegals milled outside the conference room's glass double doors. "Oh, the troops are waiting for us," said Faustina. She motioned for them to come in.

"Can't wait for our drink date tonight," said Grace as laughter and voices started to fill the conference room.

"I'm sure you can't," said Faustina. "I'm sure you can't."

Chapter Three

THE MAN CLOSED HIS apartment door and entered the cool morning. He stretched his legs and twirled his arms in three clockwise circles. The man took a deep breath, put on his hoodie, and then started on his run. He turned left on Hurlbut Street toward Pasadena Avenue and then turned left again. The man let his legs stretch out in long strides as his muscles slowly warmed up. Running cleared his mind, made him feel whole. Today, his arms and legs moved as they should, as part of one machine that was created to function without a hitch, in perfect rhythm. This was not always the case, but this time, the man felt the kind of balance that calmed a desperate small voice in his head. His breathing grew heavy as his legs moved faster and faster in the cool morning. The man's mind was free and clear as he ran and ran and ran.

TRANSCRIPT OF OVAL OFFICE MEETING, SEPT. 16, 3:35 P.M.

POTUS:	Okay, so what ya got?
ESKANDARI:	Um…
POTUS:	Big picture.
ESKANDARI:	Big picture, okay, overall, the polling looks to be…
VAN GELDEREN:	Upward trend.
ESKANDARI:	Upward trend, yes, overall.
LUNDGREN:	[UNINTELLIGIBLE]
POTUS:	How much?
LUNDGREN:	One to two points, depending on which aggregate.
POTUS:	One to two points?
ESKANDARI:	The RealClearPolitics average has us up one point in the generic two weeks after you signed the bill.
TOMA:	And FiveThirtyEight… Nate Silver… has us up two points on average.
POTUS:	Fuck Nate Silver.
ESKANDARI:	Right, er, CNN and the others put us someplace in between.
POTUS:	That's it?
ESKANDARI:	Um…
POTUS:	One to two points?
VAN GELDEREN:	On average, depending on…
POTUS:	We're less than two fucking months from the midterms.
ESKANDARI:	But the trend is upward…

POTUS:	Less than two fucking months! You all said this bill would turbocharge our poll numbers.
TOMA:	I don't think we said "turbocharge…"
POTUS:	Whatever the fuck you said. I do not want to be a goddamned lame duck with a Congress that's going to block every motherfucking thing I do including my judicial picks. I need to keep both houses, and at least the Senate because—God forbid—Justice What's-the-Fuck-His-Name goes ahead and dies on me. And then what are we going to fucking do when a new Senate that my party no longer controls gets their slimy hands on any nominee I send over? You know what's going to happen! Nada, zilch, a big nothing because the new majority leader—who likely will be No-Chin Fuck-Face—won't even let my nominees out of committee. You know that, I know that, my motherfucking shoes know that. So without the Senate to confirm my judges, who knows who's going to be president after me, and there goes my goddamn legacy.
ESKANDARI:	But the VP looks to be the only viable candidate after your second term ends. He'd continue your legacy.
POTUS:	Ha! If I were a betting woman, it won't be Vice President Shithead who'll get our motherfucking party's nomination,

because voters in the primaries are stupider than fuck. If we don't find a way to pump up our midterm poll numbers, I am royally fucked, and it will be your collective motherfucking fault! Fucked. Right. Up. My. Puckered. White. Ass.

LUNDGREN: There's still time…

POTUS: There's not a lot of fucking time.

ESKANDARI: We can hit the Sunday shows harder, and cable too. Social media, of course.

LUNDGREN: And maybe *60 Minutes*. Certainly Fox News. And you did great in your first run with that Anderson Cooper interview.

POTUS: [UNINTELLIGIBLE]

VAN GELDEREN: Maybe get the vice president to do more…

POTUS: No, I don't want Shithead out there on this. Did you see him on Meet the Press? A motherfucking disaster! He was sweating up a shitstorm. Looked like he was singlehandedly solving our drought the way he was gushing sweat everywhere, like Old Faithful! And he couldn't get a goddamned word out straight, and then…

ESKANDARI: He wasn't that bad…

POTUS: And then—and then—his fucking stutter broke loose and I couldn't fucking understand a goddamned fucking word he was saying. No, Vice President Shithead stays on the sidelines on this one!

TOMA: There is an angle we haven't pushed yet…

ESKANDARI: Right, the numbers look good on this…

POTUS:	What? What angle?
VAN GELDEREN:	We've already pushed the morality thing…
LUNDGREN:	And the economic point…
POTUS:	But?
ESKANDARI:	We haven't pushed hard, yet, on the law-and-order angle.
LUNDGREN:	And our initial polling looks strong on that…
POTUS:	How strong?
LUNDGREN:	Kind of off the charts.
POTUS:	Why the fuck have you been hiding this?
VAN GELDEREN:	We didn't have the numbers until yesterday.
ESKANDARI:	Just came in last night…
POTUS:	How do we push the law-and-order angle? I mean, it can't be that hard, right? We have these fucking Frankensteins running amok, destroying America…
TOMA:	You mean Frankenstein's monsters.
POTUS:	What?
TOMA:	You said Frankensteins running amok, but Dr. Victor Frankenstein was—in the novel—the creator of the monster. Or maybe we should say "creature" rather than "monster"—it's a less loaded term.
ESKANDARI:	Dude, stop it…
TOMA:	Anyway, as Professor Eileen M. Hunt explains in her seminal book, *Artificial Life After Frankenstein*, the doctor and his creation were quickly conflated under the sole moniker of "Frankenstein" in

	the many stage adaptations that immediately followed the novel's publication in England and France, and that conflation has continued through today.
POTUS:	What the fuck?
TOMA:	It's a common mistake, you know, erroneously using the term "Frankenstein" to refer to the creature rather than his creator. So to be correct, you really meant Frankenstein's creatures running amok destroying America—since you were using the plural—but not Frankensteins running amok.
POTUS:	What the fuck do I care? I mean, really. I don't give a flying fuck. It's a motherfucking monster named Frankenstein, okay? That's what normal people think.
TOMA:	But…
ESKANDARI:	Toma, shut it.
LUNDGREN:	Really, Toma, let it go.
TOMA:	But…
POTUS:	What was your goddamn major in college? English?
TOMA:	Well, actually, yes.
POTUS:	And look how far that got you.
TOMA:	[UNINTELLIGIBLE]
POTUS:	Someone tell me about the havoc being caused by these violent marauding Frankensteins! There has to be something!
LUNDGREN:	Yes, right…
ESKANDARI:	There have been some stories…

LUNDGREN: Police reports, here and there…
POTUS: Like what? What stories?
TOMA: Nothing totally solid, no arrests, yet…
POTUS: I don't give a shit. What kind of stories?
LUNDGREN: A few shovings…
POTUS: Shovings?
ESKANDARI: You, know, stitchers getting a little rough with people…
POTUS: Rough? How rough? This could be good shit!
LUNDGREN: Like I said, a few shovings, you know, pushing… physical stuff… reacting to people who recognize them as stitchers…
POTUS: Physical stuff?
TOMA: Short fuse, quick to anger, that kind of stuff.
POTUS: Broken bones? Cracked skulls?
TOMA: No, just roughed-up folks, harsh words exchanged, pretty unpleasant.
POTUS: Shit. Can you imagine if someone died?
LUNDGREN: That would be bad…
POTUS: Our fucking numbers would go through the fucking roof!
TOMA: But no deaths yet.
LUNDGREN: No deaths, just shovings.
POTUS: Okay, okay, we can work with this. This is good shit. Make America safe again, am I right? It worked for my reelection, and it can work again for the midterms. I can't continue my fight without keeping my majorities. That's the message!

VAN GELDEREN: We can track down stories, maybe tape some interviews.

TOMA: Maybe get some cell phone video.

POTUS: Now we're talking…

LUNDGREN: I have leads on a couple of law firms thinking about suing some of the larger reanimation companies.

POTUS: But I put them out of business with the law…

ESKANDARI: Most of them are just repurposing to other businesses. They still have piles of cash, not to mention insurance, and new patents that spun off of the reanimation technology. So if there's still a chance of liability from some stitcher going ballistic and hurting someone, you know these plaintiff firms will file suit and get a boatload of television and influence any potential jury pool. Our party could be on the right side of this.

POTUS: Yes…

TOMA: There's a three-year statute of limitations for damages caused by any of these stitchers. There haven't been any lawsuits up until now—which is pretty shocking, really, considering how some people feel about stitchers. There really haven't been any real problems, until recently, with those shovings. But maybe your signing the bill has the stitchers nervous.

POTUS: So now I'm to fucking blame? I was the

one who offered the only goddamn fix!
Everyone else started to love these motherfucking stitchers. Community meetings,
handouts, unionization, college scholar-
ships. And those college courses! Oh my
fucking God! Reanimation studies popping up in California and New Mexico
and motherfucking Arizona of all places.
Everyone was falling for their sob story.
Except me. I never liked them. I never
trusted them. My son started dating one,
but I put an end to that. It's amazing how
threatening to cut someone out of your
will can bring about a little common
sense, even to my loser son. So don't lay
this at my feet. I'm not to fucking blame
because these stitchers are beginning to
go off the rails. That's not on me! I was
the one who told the Senate and House to
pass that anti-stitcher bill. And I was the
one who signed it. I am not the problem. I
am the solution!

ESKANDARI: No, no. Of course. We can spin it a different way. We can spin it as something that
was bound to happen. And you could say
I told you so.

TOMA: You know, if you play God, see what
you get...

ESKANDARI: Law of unintended consequences...

POTUS: Okay, then we [UNINTELLIGIBLE]

VAN GELDEREN: Right, we can ride the law-and-order

	theme on the cable shows, maybe cut some commercials, and maybe we can write an op-ed for you about how you've made the country a safer place, and all that…
POTUS:	Fucking right…
TOMA:	This could really turbocharge the midterm polls…
POTUS:	Fucking right…
ESKANDARI:	We can start now…
TOMA:	We can stop work on those other spots and focus on this.
POTUS:	Go now. End of fucking meeting. Turbocharge our fucking numbers. And remember…
ESKANDARI:	Remember?
POTUS:	Keep our stuttering vice president shithead away from this.
ESKANDARI:	Got it.

—END OF TRANSCRIPT—

Chapter Four

THE MAN ENTERED THE Walgreens and strode to the back of the store where the pharmacy counter was situated near the vitamins, supplements, and various low-sugar diet aids for diabetics. He saw the line and was surprised at how many people had already queued up. Usually if he came here in the morning before work—as he had that day—he could beat the late-morning rush. Luckily, the line moved relatively fast. After fifteen minutes of waiting, only one person remained ahead of him.

The man looked up at the fluorescent lights that buzzed softly but relentlessly. He counted the number of tiles that surrounded the rectangular light fixture. *One, two, three, four, five, six, seven, eight, nine, ten.* An even ten. Three on the long sides of the rectangle, two each on the short sides. The man blinked and looked down again at the young woman who chatted with the pharmacist, a bit too friendly, as she held a bagged prescription. She already had her order. Why chat up the pharmacist and delay everyone else behind her in line? The man considered clearing his throat to let the young woman know that others were waiting, patiently, to pick up their prescriptions with no intention of chatting up the pharmacist. But would she find such a signal of impatience to be nothing short of rude or entitled? Perhaps the man should wait quietly and not say anything. Or he could speak up politely in a soft, non-entitled voice, because the young woman had her bagged prescription ready to go. Just as the man considered his options, he felt a little hand grab his right hand. The man looked down.

"Hi," said a little boy.

"Hi," said the man.

"Timothy!" said the woman who stood near the boy. "Stop bothering the man!"

The boy clung tighter to the man's hand.

"I am so sorry," said the woman. "He doesn't normally warm to strangers."

"That's okay," said the man. "He's not really bothering me."

"Timothy, one more time: let go of the man's hand," said the woman.

"But Mom," said the boy. "His hands are different."

"Of course they're different," said the woman. "Your hands are small, and his are big."

"No," said the boy. "That's not what I meant."

The man suddenly pulled his hand away from the boy. The boy started to cry.

"Timothy," said the woman, "please apologize to the man."

The boy sniffled and covered his eyes.

"I am so sorry," said the woman.

The man did not respond. He turned to face the pharmacist, who was still chatting with the young woman.

"His hands are different from each other," the boy finally explained.

The woman stiffened and looked down at the man's hands. The man shifted from one foot to the other and quickly slid his hands into his pants pockets, but it was too late: the woman let out a small, strange noise that was a cross between a gasp and a cough. The man could feel the woman staring at him, so he didn't move and kept his eyes focused straight ahead on the pharmacist.

"Let's come back a different time," said the woman. "Come on, Timothy."

The man listened to the woman's hurried footsteps as she scurried away with her son.

The young woman and the pharmacist finally finished their conversation.

"Next," said the pharmacist.

The man came up to the counter and gave his name. The pharmacist nodded and went back to the bins of prepared prescriptions. The man counted the bins: six across, five from floor to ceiling. Thirty bins total. The pharmacist found the correct prescription and brought it back to the counter. The man smiled. Finally, something was going to plan. But then the pharmacist studied the plastic bottle.

"I am so sorry," said the pharmacist.

"Why?" said the man.

"We can only partially fill your prescription—about half of this medication for you—not the usual three-month supply."

"Why?"

"There's been a run on this medication ever since, you know…"

"Ever since what?"

The pharmacist looked down at the counter. The man waited for an answer.

"Ever since the president signed that law, you know?"

The man understood which law the pharmacist meant. But he was still confused about why that would endanger his prescription's supply.

"And how does that affect my medication's availability?" said the man.

"Well, there's been a run on it, a hoarding, and some supply chain issues," said the pharmacist. "There's a fear that the manufacturers will stop making the drug. You know, rumors and stuff."

"But I still need it—we still need it—even though the president signed that law," said the man as he attempted to remain calm. He grew hot and perspiration formed on his upper lip. He knew this feeling. *Panic.*

"It will sort itself out," said the pharmacist in a gentle voice, as if calming a newborn. "I'm sure all of this will blow over in a week or two, and the supply will loosen up again. Plus, there will likely be a generic soon. Anyway, you don't have to pay until you pick up the rest of your supply."

"Yes," said the man. "Okay. Thank you."

"You're very welcome," said the pharmacist as he dropped the plastic bottle into a small white paper bag and stapled it closed.

The man grabbed the medication and turned to leave the pharmacy. As he approached the exit, he saw the woman and her child waiting by the magazine rack. The woman thumbed through a magazine. The little boy looked up at the man, smiled, and held up his hands—fingers splayed—perhaps to encourage the man to do the same so that the boy could see the anomaly again. The man averted his eyes and quickened his stride. He felt his throat closing, and he gulped at the cool air as he left the pharmacy.

The man found his car and got in. He put his prescription bag on the passenger seat, closed his eyes, and rubbed his temples. The man thought about what the pharmacist had said, that it all would work itself out, everything would be fine, maybe even a generic was on its way to being developed. But what if the pharmacist was wrong or simply lied to get the man to leave and not cause a scene? What would he do if he ran out of pills? The man could feel his heart beating in his chest. None of it seemed right or fair. Things were going well. And he had met Faustina. But none of it would matter if he ran out of pills. The man would have to tell Faustina that without his pills—well, you know—there wasn't much of a future. She'd likely feel sorry for the man but not enough to stay with him out of pity, just enough to offer him supportive words; then she'd probably ghost him, disappear.

The man opened his eyes and blinked. *Okay*, he told himself. *I have enough pills for now. I have to keep going. Stop thinking about the worst-case scenario. Faustina is in the here and now. And at this moment, I need to get to work. I have a job. I have people who rely on me. And I have a new person in my life, and I will not jump to conclusions about anything.* With this last thought, the man started his car, slowly backed out of his spot, and eased himself toward the parking lot's exit. *I have to keep going*, he thought again. *I have no choice.*

Chapter Five

BARNEY'S BEANERY WAS CROWDED for a Tuesday. Faustina had been here before for karaoke night on a Friday several months ago, and it was packed then, but that was to be expected for the beginning of the weekend. Old Town Pasadena continued to thrive, if this bar was any indication. The crowd energized Faustina and was yet another confirmation that her decision to move the law firm out of Century City to Pasadena two years ago was a prescient choice. Besides, her house in South Pasadena was but three miles away, so she no longer suffered that ungodly commute to the west side each morning.

"One sour apple martini for you," said the waiter as he gingerly placed a coaster in front of Faustina before setting down her drink.

"Thank you," said Faustina as her mouth watered in anticipation.

"And a vodka stinger for the young lady," said the waiter as he repeated the process.

"Merci beaucoup," said Grace. "And thank you for noticing my relative youth."

The waiter smiled, nodded, and went to another table to take an order.

"Vodka stinger?" said Faustina. "Are we in a Sondheim musical?"

"We are the furthest thing from those 'ladies who lunch.'"

"True."

"But you're right about the Sondheim reference."

They lifted their glasses, both approving their respective choice of libation.

"I am?"

"Yes," said Grace. "I've always wondered what they tasted like after seeing that revival of *Company* last year at the Pasadena Playhouse. So tonight I will decide for myself if it bears repeating."

"So adventurous."

"Here's to new adventures!" said Grace. She clinked her glass with Faustina's.

"New adventures!"

They each took a sip. Faustina smiled and closed her eyes in appreciation of her beverage. Grace shivered and grimaced with hers.

"Oh God," said Grace. "This might not be a great idea."

"Your new adventure is not so tasty?"

"It might take some getting used to."

"Sometimes you have to work harder to truly enjoy good things."

"I will try my best," said Grace. She took another sip and coughed as she swallowed.

"That's my girl."

"Okay, enough chitchat," said Grace after she recovered from her drink. "Spill the beans."

"Don't be racist."

"Touché," said Grace as she took another sip which produced another grimace. "But unlike your racist feng shui reference earlier today, I am completely innocent. We're at Barney's Beanery. Get it? Beans? Spill them. Tell me about this cute paralegal of yours."

"He is more handsome than cute," said Faustina. "A puppy dog is cute. A lamb is cute. Even my suit is cute. This guy is handsome."

"Tall, dark, and handsome."

"True that."

They sipped their drinks.

"I'm getting used to this," said Grace.

"Good girl," said Faustina. "I knew you could do it. You have true grit!"

"Okay, enough avoidance. I will be 30 percent happier if you spill some juicy details. Let's get real."

"Fine, shoot," said Faustina as she readied herself for Grace's interrogation. "Ask away. I want you to be 30 percent happier."

"How is it being… you know… intimate with a… a…"

"Paralegal? Oh, just fine. All his body parts work just like he was a full-fledged lawyer."

"Oh, you know what I mean," said Grace. "I noticed his hands at the Yosemite conference. I put one and one together and got two."

"That's why you're such a great lawyer, Grace. Nothing escapes you. Not even mismatched hands on a tall, handsome paralegal."

They both chuckled and fell into silence as they attended to their drinks. The crowd grew louder, the atmosphere warmer.

"I've always wondered what it would be like to be with one," said Grace. "You know, they're kind of a clean slate."

"Clean slate?"

"Yeah, you know, how the reanimation process sort of wipes them, you know, of their histories. Kind of an unavoidable side effect."

"Oh, right," said Faustina, nodding. "Anderson Cooper did this whole story on that just before Cadwallader signed that bill."

"Yeah, I saw that too," said Grace. "How the hell old is Cooper now? He still looks pretty good."

"There's a benefit to going gray young. No one notices when you actually get old."

"Yep."

"Anyway, like Cooper said, it's not a complete wipe," said Faustina. "They're left with their basic personality and the things they learned to function in this world. Plus whatever education they had too."

"But a person is not just a personality and education, right?"

"True, so that's why they can't go back to their old lives. They wouldn't have any connection to their families. When they signed the donor card, they agreed to the whole process, including the relocation program. Plus a little plastic surgery and a bit of vocal cord and fingerprint modification so they won't be recognized by a family member or otherwise be connected with their old identity. And the families get proper written notice that the body won't be coming home, plus a nice little stipend for their troubles. Anyway, it sets up the reanimated for a new life to 'invigorate the economy' or whatever they said to get government funding when they started this."

"Sounds like you've been doing a little research," said Grace.

"No comment," said Faustina. "Anyway, the safeguards make sense, don't they?"

"But the poor families don't have a body to bury."

"They usually bury some belonging that was important to the family member who agreed to be in the reanimation program. Or they do just do a memorial service. But yeah, it must be hard no matter what. And I don't think the recent ban on reanimation is going to change anything for those who already went through the process."

Faustina drained her sour apple martini and signaled for the waiter to bring two more.

"I'm not even halfway done with my vodka stinger," said Grace in her best mock-whine.

"You're a pro. You'll catch up in no time."

The waiter deposited two fresh drinks on their table and snatched away Faustina's empty glass.

"Look, I've had two nice evenings and mornings with him," said Faustina as she started on her new drink. "I'm not looking for a husband. Been there, done that. But you're right. Something feels a little…"

"A little what?"

Faustina thought for a moment, searching for the right words. Finally, she said, "A couple of weeks ago I spent time with Mom while she was recovering from that pacemaker procedure. Saul was out at the hardware store where he loves to browse, and it gave him time to stop worrying so much about Mom because I was there. Anyway, with Saul out of the house, Mom felt comfortable reminiscing about Pop and family stuff."

"Saul is a sweetie," said Grace. "I'm sure he wouldn't mind hearing those stories. I mean, your mom and dad were married a long, long time. Saul does not begrudge her that. And besides, Saul had been married a long time too. Husbands and wives pass away. That's part of life."

"You're right, Saul is a sweetie and he wouldn't mind, but Mom would, you know—Catholic guilt," said Faustina.

"Combine that with Saul's Jewish guilt, and you've got quite a combo."

Faustina chuckled. "Anyway, I guess Mom was really feeling her mortality even though she's one tough lady."

"To raise a chingona like you, she has to be tough."

"You're damn right. Anyway, this last time, as Mom started telling me about her parents' courtship as well as her own early life with Pop, I suddenly realized something that connected her stories with my own life in LA."

"Yes?" said Grace as she warmed to her vodka stinger. She drained her glass, set it down, and picked up her fresh drink.

"It turns out my family has had key personal events happen over the last century on a three-block stretch of Spring Street downtown."

"That's crazy! In a city this big?"

"I know, right? First, as for my grandparents, literally a hundred years ago, they had known each other in Mexico as teenagers but migrated separately to California, because my grandmother was fed up with my grandfather's roaming eye and refusal to commit."

"Men," said Grace.

"Then at a New Year's party held at the Alexandria Hotel on Spring Street, they reunited and my grandfather decided to settle down and marry my grandmother," said Faustina.

"And second?"

"And second, just down the street, the Title Insurance and Trust Building one block away played a role in my parents' life.

Mom explained that when she graduated from Saint Agnes High School, she became a secretary in that building. Pop had been her high school sweetheart, but he had enlisted because jobs were scarce and he figured he could get some benefits. After a two-year stint based in San Diego, he returned and landed a job at a factory in Watts, and they started dating again. During this time, Mom would have lunchtime calls with Pop at the public payphone outside her building right there on Spring Street. And it was during one of those phone calls that my father proposed."

"How romantic," said Grace. "You're going to make me cry."

"I might make myself cry. It's so sweet, isn't it?"

"And payphones? Oh, things were so simple back then. No texting."

"And little did that beautiful young couple know that their only child would go to law school and eventually work as a young lawyer for the California Department of Justice in the Reagan State Building one block down from where Mom had worked."

"Your first real job, right?"

Faustina grinned. "Yep, I cut my litigation teeth as a government lawyer in the Land Use and Conservation Section. But the point is, I told my mom that it's amazing to me that a three-block stretch of Spring Street has played a key role in our family's history for a full century."

"Oh my God, that's true!"

They both smiled and took a sip from their drinks.

"But how is that relevant to the question at hand?" said Grace.

"What was the question?"

"Well, I guess there wasn't a question per se, more of a plea for you to spill the beans."

"Don't be racist."

"Enough!" said Grace. "I am now officially pissed with you, my friend. Connect the dots for me, por favor."

"Well, you said it yourself: a reanimated person is a clean slate. They have no history, at least nothing they can remember. And here I am with all of this history going back generations just in LA alone, not even counting all of my family's history in Mexico."

"So?"

"So even though he's a nice guy and I've enjoyed some time with him, I have a history and he doesn't," said Faustina.

"What do you mean?"

Faustina took a drink. "Let me think of the right words…"

"You who are so good with words."

"Okay, I think I've got it," said Faustina. "How can you have a future without a past?"

"So existential of you," said Grace. "But sometimes a past can leave pretty bad damage. There are a few things I'd like to wipe from my memory. Past is prologue and all that."

"And there's another problem," said Faustina as she signaled for the waiter to bring the check.

"What's that?"

"The reanimation only lasts twenty years, max. As long as they take their medication. And they can't repeat the process, so there's no chance for adding years."

"So? Twenty years is a long time."

"Spoken like a woman in her early thirties."

"Who looks nineteen."

"My point is," said Faustina, "what's the use of building a life with someone and getting ready for a beautiful retirement with the love of your life only to have the timer set at twenty years?"

"Most people don't stay married that long anyway," said

Grace. "You could have a torrid love affair for fifteen years, and then you catch him cheating, so you dump him and move on. In my book, that's fifteen good years."

"Oh, Grace…"

"Carpe diem," said Grace as she lifted her vodka stinger in a solo toast and then drained the last of her drink. "I can get used to these things."

"That's my girl."

"But you never told me the most important thing."

"What's that?"

"Are all of his parts mismatched?" said Grace with an exaggerated and suggestive wink.

"Oh, you bitch!" laughed Faustina. "You did not just go there."

"Oh, you bitch, I did just go there."

Faustina rolled her eyes and sat in silence.

"Well?" said Grace.

"He's pretty well matched except for that left arm," Faustina finally relented. "Otherwise, they did a pretty good job putting together the whole package."

"So with respect to the mismatched arm…"

"What?"

"Did it feel like two different guys were running their hands over your hot little body?"

Faustina snorted. "Oh dear God, Grace! How does your mind go down these strange, kinky places? Does Brandon know about your very nasty proclivities?"

"It must be the vodka stinger," said Grace. "It's loosened my inner demons and desires. Besides, Brandon knows every side of me. And I mean every."

The waiter set the tab between the two friends. Grace snatched it before Faustina knew what had happened.

"My treat," said Grace as she pulled a credit card from her purse.

"No," said Faustina. "We always go Dutch. And besides, my partnership share is much larger than yours."

"No, my friend. You officially spilled the beans—and I mean that in a nonracist way, my Chicana friend. It's the least I can do."

"Mil gracias."

"My pleasure. But we need to talk about my partnership draw sometime."

"Oops, didn't mean to open a can of worms."

"No worries," said Grace. "I don't need much more. As long as I draw more than Leonard, I will be a happy woman."

"That's for another night of drinks."

"It's a date, my friend. Not a sexy date with multiple guys wrapped into one, but a date nonetheless."

"Spare me," said Faustina. "Spare me."

FAUSTINA NORMALLY DID NOT buzz-browse for books, especially after drinking sour apple martinis, but Grace had got her thinking. What if this developed into something beyond casual dating? And what if there were pitfalls she was not prepared for? After all, relationships took work even under ideal circumstances. The whole reanimation angle was not something she'd bargained for or had wanted to think about. But Grace, of course, had to go there and focus on that. So after leaving Barney's Beanery and hugging Grace goodnight, she walked along Colorado Boulevard toward Vroman's Bookstore. Faustina had one more hour before it closed, so she walked as fast as she could considering her slightly inebriated state. She entered the bookstore and meandered toward the nonfiction section.

Faustina passed by the various literature- and art-inspired collectibles and stopped in front of the Frida Kahlo–inspired products. There were Frida Kahlo socks, coffee mugs, nesting dolls, notebooks, bookmarks, wineglasses, embroidered purses, shot glasses, dolls, kitchen mitts (one with Frida Kahlo, the other with Diego Rivera), votive candles, and on and on and on and on. Faustina shook her head. What would Frida think? She'd certainly laugh and say it was all a bunch of commercial capitalistic mierda that commodified an artist to the financial benefit of those who had no understanding of her art. ¡Tan ridículo!

Faustina continued on her mission, eventually wandering down the correct aisle and finding the section chock-full of self-help relationship books. She hated the genre. A whole industry was built on people's insecurities when, in truth, a good relationship only took hard work, honesty, and a little consideration. There was nothing mysterious or magical or scientific about listening to your partner, making thoughtful choices, and communicating honestly. Hell, she could write a relationship book and make a mint. But it would only be a page long, so maybe it'd be a flop. Not enough complication, no clever chapter titles, no index or recommended reading or charts or graphs. Faustina scanned the titles, which all seemed to be smart catchphrases or puns. Book marketing was an art, no doubt. *Give the people what they want!* Clearly a lot of books were being written not out of altruism but because people were buying them. Love was a big business, the biggest of them all, bigger than the military-industrial complex. Perhaps less deadly, but certainly more irritating.

Faustina finally came to a section under a handwritten sign

that proclaimed *FOR LOVERS OF THE REANIMATED*. How unfair! Why wouldn't there be books for the reanimated under a sign that said *FOR LOVERS OF THE UN-REANIMATED*? Such implicit bias. But since she was there, Faustina examined the titles. A few of them made her laugh or groan. She eventually came to one that sounded interesting with a subtle title, *Making It Work: Loving the Reanimated in Your Life* by Dr. Elizabeth Lavenza. Faustina pulled the book, turned it over to read the back cover, and was impressed by the author's credentials—degrees from Stanford and Yale, and five best-selling self-help books. The doctor's headshot was impressive in and of itself. Staring back at Faustina was a handsome woman in her forties who had an expression of complete competence but also great empathy for her confused reading public. She opened the book and scanned the table of contents. Faustina let out a long sigh. So much work. But the book's title telegraphed that point, didn't it? She snapped the book closed and returned it to its home on the shelf.

I will use my smarts and instinct, she thought. *Who needs Dr. Stanford-Yale's help?* With that, Faustina turned and headed toward the fiction section to look for the new Urrea novel, then maybe she'd grab a café de olla and some pan dulce at the bookstore's new coffee place, Tepito. Her sour apple martinis were beginning to wear off anyway. Clearly relationship books were a buzzkill.

Chapter Six

THE MAN CLOSED HIS apartment door and entered the cool evening. He stretched his legs and twirled his arms in three clockwise circles. The man took a deep breath, put on his hoodie, and then started on his nightly run, happy to be back on his usual exercise schedule after the recent disruption. Morning runs were fine, but there was something particularly cleansing about exercising at the end of the day. He turned left on Hurlbut Street toward Pasadena Avenue and then turned left again. The man let his legs stretch out in long strides as his muscles slowly warmed up. He wanted to achieve his usual peace when he ran. But something was amiss. The man sensed that something was about to change in his life. He shook his head to chase away this feeling of unease. But he could not. He approached a crow pecking furiously at a Burger King wrapper that held delicious remnants of a hamburger bun. The crow froze and looked up at the man as he grew nearer. The bird did not stir even as the man moved quickly. Finally, when the man was a mere six feet away, the crow let out an angry squawk, spread its wings, flew away, and perched on a nearby wooden fence. The man passed the Burger King wrapper and then turned his head to look at the crow. The bird spread its wings and flew back to its feast. As the man returned his sight to the sidewalk ahead of him, the crow recommenced its voracious feasting on its banquet.

TELEVISION COMMERCIAL

ON-SCREEN: Grainy black-and-white video of a busy city street with crowds of people. Ominous music.

VOICEOVER: You've seen them—in your kids' classrooms and in your churches, factories, and offices. This massive tide of fake people is draining your paychecks, fueling inflation, wrecking your schools, ruining your hospitals, and threatening your families.

CUT TO: A man shoving another man, a crowd surrounding the two, some yelling, "He's a stitcher!" and "Stitcher go home!"

VOICEOVER: They're losing control and shoving people in the streets. And what's next? Are they becoming drug dealers, sex traffickers, and violent predators who freely mingle with the crowds, your coworkers, your children? You know it, we know it, everyone knows it. They bring drugs. They bring crime. They are rapists. Some are even running for Congress.

SOUNDTRACK: Ominous music switches to patriotic music.

CUT TO: President Cadwallader surrounded by Cabinet members during a signing ceremony.

VOICEOVER: But only one party had the guts to say, "Enough is enough!" By signing the

Anti-Stitcher Law, your president took a vital step in protecting you and your children. But without the right Congress, the president's successes will be defeated. Your vote matters more than ever before. These midterm elections are literally a matter of life and death.

CUT TO: An American flag waving.

SOUNDTRACK: Patriotic music begins to swell.

VOICEOVER: Make America safe again!

CUT TO: A close-up of President Cadwallader smiling and giving two thumbs up.

VOICEOVER: Paid for by Citizens to Make America Safe Again, fighting for a return to common sense in America, highlighting the importance of logic and reason, and defeating "wokeism" and anti–critical thinking ideologies that permeate every sector of our country and threaten the very freedoms that are foundational to the American dream.

SOUNDTRACK: Music rises to crescendo.

                  FADE TO BLACK

Chapter Seven

"NICE JOB," SAID NORMAN as he handed the brief to the man. "I made a few edits in red—okay, okay, I'm very old-school and like the red pen—but overall, you hit all of the right arguments."

The man thumbed through the brief and nodded.

"I hate putting my edits on an electronic document," continued Norman. "Nothing like the feel of a red pen on real paper, am I right?"

"I have heard that before," said the man as he continued to thumb through the brief.

"I usually bleed red all over everything I edit, but yours was in pretty good shape—didn't need that much tweaking," said Norman. "Granted, it's a relatively simple motion, but considering you hadn't written one before—and you're only a paralegal and not an attorney, no offense—this is definitely pretty good. Better than some of our young lawyers, actually."

The man looked up from the brief and nodded.

"You are what they call 'value added.'"

"Thank you," said the man.

Norman leaned back in his chair. "Motions to intervene are usually granted, but it's always better to put our best foot forward, right?"

"Yes. Best foot forward."

"Anyway, put those edits in today. And then email it back to me so I can look at it one more time before I get it over to my secretary to file and serve tomorrow morning. I love getting things in early, plus defendant's counsel is simply going to shit when she gets served with it. The last thing her clients want is having another party to litigate against."

"Yes, I will do that," said the man as he started walking out of Norman's office.

"Oh, could you close the door behind you?" said Norman.

The man nodded and closed the door as he left. Norman snorted and shook his head as he turned to his computer screen and started scrolling through emails.

"Fucking stitcher," he said. "Fucking goddamn stitcher."

THE MAN WALKED BACK to his cubicle and pulled up the intervention motion on his computer. He set the marked-up motion to the right of his keyboard and turned to the first page that had red ink on it. He examined the red ink, counted the edits on each page, then turned to the computer screen and typed in the edits. The man went through the document, page by page, meticulously reading the red edit marks and then making the changes on the computer. After he completed the edits, he emailed it to Norman. He looked at his watch and saw that it was twelve fifteen.

The man reached beneath his desk and retrieved a black lunch bag. He opened it and carefully removed its contents: a tuna sandwich on wheat bread, a bottle of water, an apple, and a granola bar. He set these lunch items on his desk in a row according to size and shape. The man then retrieved a paper napkin from his lunch bag and spread it across his lap. After taking a bite out of his sandwich, apple, and granola bar—in that order—he took a drink of water. He then turned to his computer, opened the Google page, and typed in the search engine, *good places to go on a date in Pasadena.*

The man pushed enter and watched the results appear. He got 42.6 million hits. He scratched his chin and considered his next step. There were too many options.

"Hot date planning?"

The man swiveled in his chair to see who had walked into his cubicle and asked the question. Tina leaned against the side of the cubicle wall, arms crossed, reading glasses perched on top of her head. The man nodded.

"I want to plan a date in Pasadena because that's where she lives, and she even has her office there, so I think it would be convenient in case she has to go back to the office after the date," said the man. He then turned back to the computer screen and started to scan the search results. Tina sighed, entered the cubicle, and sat on the edge of the man's desk.

"Are you going to read all 42.6 million hits?" said Tina.

"No," said the man. "I need to edit my search."

"No," said Tina. "What you need is to listen to an expert like me."

The man turned to Tina. "You're an expert on dating in Pasadena?"

"Oh, my friend, I am an expert on all things romantic."

"May I take notes?"

Tina laughed. "Yes, but everything I say is copyrighted, so don't go stealing it for your blog."

"I don't have a blog," said the man.

Tina chuckled. "I was joking."

"I see."

"Okay, before I bestow upon you my brilliant dating knowledge, what is it you want out of this date?"

"I don't understand."

Tina leaned in and whispered, "Have you two been… you know… intimate yet?"

The man leaned in and whispered, "Yes. Five times, over the course of two dates."

"Oh, you two have been frisky," laughed Tina.

The man smiled. He liked the sound of the word *frisky*.

"Okay, since you've already done the dirty deed five times with this mysterious woman whose name you clearly do not want to share since you've not mentioned it yet, how about a more cerebral date to help build on the carnal?"

The man lifted a pen to the pad of paper and gave a look to Tina that signaled he was ready to take notes.

Tina clapped her hands together. "Okay, how about a daytime date, like on a weekend, to enjoy our beautiful weather and your lady friend's beautiful mind?"

"Yes," said the man as he wrote the words *DAYTIME DATE IN PASADENA* at the top of the first sheet of paper. He then held his pen aloft, ready to record Tina's words of advice.

"So… Pasadena… Pasadena…" said Tina. "Ah! I got it. I simply love the Norton Simon Museum. Great exhibits, beautiful gardens with a pond, good food at the café, a gift shop to spend oodles of cash in, and they've got these amazing Rodins on the lawn even before you enter the main building."

"Rodins?"

"You know, Auguste Rodin. There's something like seven or eight of his sculptures on the front lawn: *The Walking Man*, *The Burghers of Calais*, *Saint John the Baptist*, *The Thinker*, and my all-time favorite, the *Monument to Balzac*. And a couple more, I think. Here, let me pull it up on your computer."

Tina gently pushed the man out of his chair, sat, and quickly found the museum's website. After a few clicks, she located the Rodin sculptures and then let the man sit again so that he could click through the images. The man methodically pulled up each image and studied the sculpture that filled the screen. His breathing slowed, and he smiled. First he clicked on *The Burghers of Calais*, then *Saint John the Baptist*, followed by *The Thinker*, and then the *Monument to Balzac*. Tina enjoyed observing the man's expressions change with each image. The man's face brightened, his eyes widened, his smile grew. He let out an *ah!* with each succeeding image. Finally the man clicked on *The Walking Man*. He fell back into his chair and shivered. Tina leaned in to examine the photograph.

"That is pretty kick-ass, actually," said Tina. "Very powerful, even with no head. Or maybe because he's missing the ol' noggin. I might change my favorite piece by good ol' Balzac to *The Walking Man*."

The man continued to stare at the image of *The Walking Man*. He did not recognize what he felt at that moment. All he knew was that his chest swelled, and his eyes moistened. At last the man finally said: "Oh."

Tina clapped. "Yes! So that is how your date begins—at the museum's entrance, where you two can be bathed in beautiful, breathtaking Rodin sculptures—and then into the museum for some brilliant art, antiquities, and more sculpture. And then after a nice late lunch in the café near the gardens out back, the happy couple can browse in the museum's bookstore. Plenty of opportunities to get to know each other, right? That's how my wife realized I was the woman for her."

"Yes," said the man as he continued staring at *The Walking Man*. "This sounds like a good idea."

"Good? Good? More like brilliant, as the British say!"

"Yes, brilliant."

"And then if you have time afterward—and to continue the theme of books—you can go to Vroman's Bookstore and browse around, including the literary tchotchkes and collectibles," said Tina. "Plus they have a wine bar there, too, which is pretty damn wonderful. The café has amazing coffee and baked goods—I love the scones, but they do have delicious pan dulce—if you want to keep alcohol out of it, which is certainly one way to go."

"That is a very good idea."

"I know," said Tina. "I am pretty fucking brilliant at this dating thing. If I weren't so happily married, I'd go on date after date after date, all perfectly planned. And if you ever have a second or third date with your special person, there are so many other wonderful bookstores to visit, both in and out of Pasadena: Octavia's Bookshelf, Tía Chucha's, Skylight Books, The Last Bookstore, Eso Won Books, Book Soup, Diesel, Libros Schmibros, LibroMobile, Other Books, MiJa Books, and on and on and on! I love bookshop dates."

"Thank you," said the man as he quickly scribbled some notes. "I will keep these in mind."

"My pleasure!" said Tina. "Our kind have got to stick together."

The man turned to Tina. "You mean paralegals?"

"That too," said Tina with a chuckle. "That too."

A jolt of recognition went through the man. Tina winked,

turned, and started to walk away. The man never suspected that Tina was reanimated. She appeared flawlessly matched from head to toe, as if born that way. He felt a pang of remorse. Why couldn't his reanimation doctor find a better match for his left arm? Imagine how much easier it would be to go through this world looking like everyone else. Normal. Just another person in a sea of people. The man sighed, and his mind went back to the helpful dating tips Tina had given him. The man smiled as his remorse receded and turned back to *The Walking Man*. He had a date to plan.

Chapter Eight

FAUSTINA AND THE MAN stood in front of the sculpture. A small brown sparrow hopped about on the lawn's edge that surrounded the sculpture's concrete base. The sun's rays broke through the eucalyptus branches and leaves to dapple the bronze with an enchanted light.

"You make us proud of our legs, old man," said Faustina.

"What?" said the man, keeping his eyes on the sculpture.

"That's from a Carl Sandburg poem about this very piece."

"Someone wrote a poem about this sculpture? That is something I did not know."

"Oh, yes, my art history degree actually serves a purpose from time to time, even if only to entertain," laughed Faustina. "But I had to go to law school to pay the rent."

They continued to admire the sculpture.

"In French, it's *L'homme qui marche*," said Faustina.

"That sounds better than *The Walking Man*," said the man.

"Everything sounds better in French."

"That is also something I did not know."

"And I bet you also didn't know that *The Walking Man* is a version of *Saint John the Baptist* over there but without a head and arms," said Faustina as she pointed to the other sculpture.

The man looked at *Saint John the Baptist* and then back to *The Walking Man* and then back to *Saint John the Baptist*. The little brown sparrow pecked at the grass three times and then flew off.

"Why would Rodin remove Saint John's head and arms to make *The Walking Man*?" the man finally asked.

"Well, some think that *The Walking Man* was a preliminary study for the complete *Saint John the Baptist*, but others think *The Walking Man* was meant to be whole unto itself, complete in its own way," said Faustina.

The man nodded in thought.

"And Rodin composed the sculpture from a fragmented torso he attached to legs that he had sculpted for a different figure. But I think it works, don't you?"

"Even with a missing head and arms?"

"Look at *The Walking Man*," said Faustina. "Would you change it if you could?"

The man studied *The Walking Man* again and thought. Finally, after a full minute of concentration, he said, "I think it's perfect the way it is."

"So you've answered your own question."

"I did."

They stood in silence, absorbing the power of *The Walking Man*.

"I often wonder how my life would have been different if I continued with art history," said Faustina. "You know, getting a masters and PhD. Maybe I'd be teaching or curating at a museum like this. Don't get me wrong. I love being a lawyer, doing environmental cases, attacking climate change, going after plastic pollution, and all that. Fighting the good fight. It's God's work, as Mom says. Plus the money ain't bad. But I sometimes think about that other life I never had. Would I have been happier? Would I be a fundamentally different person? Do you ever think that?"

"I've never thought about that."

"But I do know one thing," said Faustina. "I love this museum. Every time I'm here, I feel renewed by the art."

The man turned to Faustina. "I didn't know you'd been here before. I thought it was something new for you when I suggested it."

"Oh, I don't mind at all. I never get tired of looking at beautiful art. Besides..."

"Besides?"

"Besides," said Faustina, "I've never been here with you, so that makes it a new experience, right?"

The man thought about this observation. "Yes," he finally said, "I think you're right."

"Have you been here before?" said Faustina.

"No," said the man. "At least not that I know of."

"So in some ways I am looking at it through your eyes. So it's sort of like a new experience for me."

Faustina's phone beeped. She studied the new text. "Oh, fuck," she said.

"What's wrong," said the man.

"It's Saul, my stepfather," said Faustina as she texted a reply. "Mom is in the hospital. I've got to get there. It's the Huntington Hospital on California, so it's not too far. About five minutes away." She took a few steps toward the parking lot.

"I can go with you," said the man.

"Okay, okay, can you drive?" said Faustina. "That would help."

"Yes, I can drive."

"And we can get my car later."

"Yes," said the man. "I parked over there."

"SHE'S SLEEPING RIGHT NOW," said Saul as Faustina and the man walked quickly down the hall toward him.

Saul opened his arms to receive his stepdaughter and give her a big hug. After a few moments, they separated, and Faustina introduced the man to Saul as her friend.

"Happy to meet a friend of Faustina's," said Saul.

"Let's go to the waiting room so we can talk," said Faustina. "Just let the desk know so they can get us when they know more."

Saul dutifully complied and then the trio walked to the waiting room down the hall. They entered the small, earth-toned room, and Faustina guided Saul to a row of chairs. They all sat.

"So what do they think?" said Faustina.

"Still running tests. Since she had that pacemaker put in, she had been doing better. But this morning she was feeling out of sorts, and then I got worried about the things she was saying." Saul ran his left hand through his shaggy gray hair.

Faustina took a deep breath. "What do you mean, the things she was saying?"

"Well, she started to respond to any question I asked in, er, you know, Spanish," said Saul. "And she knows I don't speak much beyond a few phrases. I never was any good with languages."

"Oh, shit."

"Yeah, so maybe a stroke. They don't know yet."

"Did she slur?" said Faustina.

"A little, but not much. As far as I could tell, her sentences made sense, but like I said, I'm not the best judge of that. I asked her what day it was and what my name was, you know, all the things they say you should ask if you think someone has had a stroke. Those AARP newsletters actually have good articles in them, especially about health. Anyway, she was lucid and knew the answers to all of my questions. The doctor said it could just be that she was dehydrated or just tired. You know, we're not getting any younger."

"Have you eaten anything?" said Faustina.

"I had a few spoonsful of oatmeal and a sip of coffee, but I got worried about your mother so I decided to bring her here and worry about breakfast later."

Faustina turned toward the man. "Would you mind running over to the cafeteria to get a coffee and a muffin or something for Saul? I don't want to leave in case they get news about Mom."

"I can do that," said the man. He then paused. "Do you want something too?"

Faustina smiled. "A coffee would be great."

"With half-and-half," said the man.

"Yes, with half-and-half," said Faustina.

"I take mine black," said Saul, offering a tired smile. "Thank you much."

"You're welcome," said the man as he stood and then left the waiting room.

"So how are you?" said Saul. "New boyfriend? He knows how you take your coffee."

"Saul, I'm almost forty."

"Okay, significant other? Partner? Reason for living? Booty call?"

Faustina let out a guffaw and then a snort.

"So ladylike," laughed Saul.

"He's just a guy I've been spending time with recently, that's all."

"He seems nice."

"He is."

"Does your mother know about him yet?"

"No, I wasn't ready. It's all too new. Maybe it won't last."

Saul put his arm around Faustina. "Any guy would be lucky to have your heart."

Faustina leaned into Saul. "That's why Mom fell for you after Pop died. You're a sweetie."

They sat in silence, listening to themselves breathe, both lost in thought.

"So," said Saul, "I did notice."

"What did you notice?" said Faustina as she extricated herself from Saul's arm.

"You know, his hands."

"And?"

"And nothing, really," said Saul. "Forget I said anything."

"Do you think it's an issue?"

"No, no, not at all. I just noticed."

Faustina shifted in her seat. "It's not a big deal."

"Look," said Saul as he patted Faustina's arm, "it's not a big deal. The most important thing is that you're happy. There's just so much hatred out there. But you know the risks."

"I do."

"So don't worry about an old man's concerns. You will be fine. You always are."

"It's not serious. I mean, it's all too new to know if it's going to get serious, so it's not a big deal, okay?"

"I'm sorry, dear, I wasn't trying to upset you. I'll stay out of your business. Let's focus on your mom, okay?"

Faustina leaned back in her chair and crossed her arms. She stared at the wallpaper across the room. The design bothered her in all its bland, noncontroversial glory: brown and tan leaves gently falling from an unseen tree. Who could create such eye pablum? The artist likely studied at one of the finest art schools but could only get work in the commercial wallpaper industry. A person wearing blue scrubs walked into the room, disrupting Faustina's musings.

"Mr. Saperstein?"

"Yes," said Saul as he stood.

"I'm Dr. Yi," she said, nodding. "Your wife is awake and she's doing much better. Dr. Ralston, whom you met when your wife was admitted, briefed me earlier before I started my rounds."

Faustina stood and said, "Was it a stroke?"

"You're her daughter?"

"Yes."

"I see the resemblance," said the doctor with a smile. "No stroke. She was dehydrated. I have her on an IV of saline to rehydrate her, and also we'll be adjusting her diuretics. This is common for someone her age, and she just had that pacemaker put in. But it might be wise to keep her here overnight until she's stable and we've ruled everything else out."

"Makes sense," said Faustina.

"May we see her?" said Saul.

"Give her about fifteen minutes," said the doctor. "The nurse is finishing up with her right now."

"Okay," said Saul. "Okay. Thank you, Doctor."

"My pleasure." She nodded and left.

Saul and Faustina sighed in unison and sat again. The man came back into the waiting room carrying two paper cups of coffee. A blueberry muffin wrapped in cellophane balanced on the cup's plastic lid.

"Okay, now you eat something," said Faustina. "You have to keep up your strength to take care of Mom."

"Yes, boss," said Saul. "That is my sole goal in life."

"MIJA, I AM FINE," said Verónica. "Stop fussing."

"Mom," said Faustina as she leaned over her mother, "you were speaking Spanish to Saul and you know he doesn't speak it. So of course he knew something was wrong."

"Maybe I wanted to teach him a new language."

Saul laughed and winked at Verónica.

"Lo siento," said Verónica to the man. "This is not the way I wanted to meet my daughter's new novio."

"He is not my new novio," said Faustina.

The man looked at Faustina and then back to Verónica.

"Let him speak for himself," said Verónica. "What are you? A new novio, or just a friend?"

The man looked at Verónica. Faustina was simply a younger version of this woman, whose age and medical situation did nothing to diminish her beauty.

"Objection," said Faustina. She turned to the man and stage-whispered, "Your attorney advises you not to answer that question."

"I am a man," said the man.

Verónica let out a little laugh. "Sí, veo que eres un hombre."

"Sí, solo soy un hombre," said the man.

Faustina turned to the man. "You speak Spanish?"

"Yes," said the man. "A little."

"I didn't know that," said Faustina.

"You didn't ask," said the man in a gentle tone.

Verónica smiled and nodded.

"¿Dónde naciste?" said Verónica.

The man thought. He assumed he was born in three different places—judging by the map of his body—but he didn't know where because that information was never shared. But he did know that his reanimation was done in a facility located north of Los Angeles in Oxnard.

"Oxnard," said the man.

"Ellos cultivan fresas en Oxnard," said Verónica.

"Yes," said Faustina, training her eyes on the man. "They grow the best strawberries there."

The man nodded. A memory lurked in the shadows of his mind, but it quickly slipped away.

"Oh, crap," said Faustina as her phone beeped. She read her calendar alert to herself. "I completely forgot that Leonard and his hubby are hosting our annual firm party tonight. I shouldn't go, not with Mom here and all."

"No, Mija," said Verónica. "You and your new novio should go. I am doing fine. No te preocupes. Saul is here. The doctors and nurses are nice."

"Everything is under control here," said Saul. "They're going to kick you out anyway at eight, probably right around the time the party would be starting. You two should go. They're keeping your mom overnight anyway, and there's only room for me to sack out there on that recliner."

"I didn't know about this party," said the man.

Faustina blushed. "It's not a big deal. I wasn't going to bother you about it since we had our… our… trip to the museum anyway. You'd be sick of me."

"But…" said the man.

"We can talk about it later."

"But I would like to meet your friends."

Faustina almost jumped. She looked at the man. Verónica smiled. Saul tried unsuccessfully to muffle a chuckle.

"You and your new novio should go to the party tonight," said Verónica. "That would make me happy."

"Oh, okay," said Faustina. "But we need to get my car from the museum, and I want to shower and change into something nicer."

"Yes," said the man. "That makes sense. And I want to go for a run anyway, so I'll need to shower too."

Saul clapped his hands together. "Sounds like a plan! Again, don't worry. Your mom is stronger than all of us put together. You two have fun, and then Faustina can call me tomorrow morning so I can give you an update. And we all have cell phones, so we are all connected. We mean it. Have fun. Deal?"

"Deal," said Faustina as she leaned down to kiss her mother. "Deal."

THEY SAT IN SILENCE as the man guided his car back to the museum's parking lot. He carefully pulled into a spot that had just opened up near Faustina's car. The man parked but left the motor running. He looked to his left and could see the torso of *The Walking Man*, the lower half of the sculpture obfuscated by a black Mercedes. The man thought about what Faustina had told him about the sculpture. It was perfect, even with no head or arms. He wouldn't change a thing about it.

"You know, you don't have to go to the law firm party," said Faustina. "Don't feel compelled just because my mother basically invited you."

The man turned toward Faustina. "I want to go," he said. He thought for a moment. Then he said, "Do you want me to go?"

Faustina laughed. "That's the million-dollar question, right?"

The man turned back toward *The Walking Man*. The black Mercedes backed out so that the lower part of the sculpture gradually became visible.

"I don't understand," said the man. "What's the million-dollar question?"

"What are we?"

"What do you mean?"

They sat in silence again. The man could now see the whole of *The Walking Man*. He could not take his eyes of the Rodin sculpture.

"You know," ventured Faustina, "if you meet my friends, certain expectations are created. Right?"

"Like what?"

Faustina sighed. "Like they think we're a couple or something."

"I met your mother and stepfather," said the man as he turned away from *The Walking Man* and focused on his dashboard.

"You have a point," laughed Faustina. "Oh, fuck it. We'll have fun. I'm the senior partner, goddamn it. It will be fine."

"Yes, it will be fine."

"And if my lawyer friends want to assume a fact not in evidence, then that's their problem."

Faustina opened the car door and paused. "Like I said, I'm going to take a short nap, then shower and change. I can swing by your place around seven."

"Yes, I will be ready. I have time to go for a run and shower."

"And don't snack too much between now and then. Leonard cooks up a storm. I have a nice bottle of pinot grigio chilling in the fridge that I can bring. You don't need to bring anything since I invited you."

"I will see you at seven," said the man as he glanced at *The Walking Man* one more time before turning to Faustina. "I will not snack too much."

"Famous last words," said Faustina as she got out of the car. "See you in a few hours, okay?"

"Yes, three hours and twenty-two minutes," said the man as he scanned the time on his dashboard.

Faustina laughed. "You are quite precise, my friend."

"Yes," said the man. "I am."

Chapter Nine

THE MAN CLOSED HIS apartment door and entered the cool but sunny late afternoon. He stretched his legs and twirled his arms in three clockwise circles. The man took a deep breath, put on his hoodie, and then started on his run. He turned left on Hurlbut Street toward Pasadena Avenue and then turned left again. The man let his legs stretch out in long strides as his muscles slowly warmed up. He concentrated on his breathing. But the differences in his arms started to break his concentration. His longer left arm felt disconnected from the rest of his body. The man stopped and held out his arms in front of him. He shook his head, sighed, and let out an almost imperceptible moan.

ABC WORLD NEWS TONIGHT
INTERVIEW WITH ELOISE MILLER,
SECRETARY OF HEALTH AND HUMAN SERVICES

DAVID MUIR:	Thank you for joining us this evening, Secretary Miller.
ELOISE MILLER:	My pleasure.
DAVID MUIR:	Last month, President Cadwallader signed the anti-reanimation bill as the capstone of her domestic agenda before the midterm elections, hailed it as a great victory for the American people and human decency, and declared that the special interests lost.
ELOISE MILLER:	Yes, the president is absolutely right . . .
DAVID MUIR:	But we're the only country that's banned reanimation, and there are reports that China, India, Russia, and other countries are ramping up their reanimation programs with an eye toward beefing up their factories and even their militaries. So how can this new law be a major victory for the American people when it's going to put us behind other countries?
ELOISE MILLER:	That's not the way to look at it. As the president said, this is about human decency and fighting special interests . . .
DAVID MUIR:	But didn't the president really just cave to special interests that were against reanimation from the beginning?

ELOISE MILLER: Well, no, there are special interests and
                    then there are special interests. There's
                    a difference.

DAVID MUIR: What does that mean?

ELOISE MILLER: I mean, the president listened to those
                    valid concerns about stitchers . . .

DAVID MUIR: I'm sorry to interrupt, Secretary Miller,
                    but many consider that a derogatory term,
                    a slur.

ELOISE MILLER: And that's another problem we're fight-
                    ing against: political correctness. We can't
                    be afraid to call a spade a spade.

DAVID MUIR: But the reanimated community is made
                    up of people . . .

ELOISE MILLER: Sometimes multiple people wrapped into
                    one . . .

DAVID MUIR: Back to my question. How is this a victory
                    when other countries will continue—and
                    even ramp up—reanimation programs?

ELOISE MILLER: Well, if the president maintains her par-
                    ty's majorities in the House and Senate,
                    she will ask for additional legislation to be
                    sent to her desk and also look at executive
                    order options.

DAVID MUIR: What kind?

ELOISE MILLER: We can't stop other countries' stitcher
                    programs completely, but we can impose
                    sanctions as well as ban stitcher travel
                    into our country.

DAVID MUIR: A travel ban?

ELOISE MILLER: The president has always asserted that

we need to beef up our borders, and she's made a lot of headway on that already. But more can be done.

DAVID MUIR: Wouldn't that be counterproductive and just play into the growing anti-reanimation bias?

ELOISE MILLER: The president has been clear: we need to make America safe again. The MASA movement is strong and will carry us to victory in the midterms.

DAVID MUIR: But there is, unsurprisingly, a growing movement in the reanimation community for civil rights protections because they are people.

ELOISE MILLER: Are they really?

DAVID MUIR: Their DNA says they are.

ELOISE MILLER: Well, that's just science-speak. In reality, whether they are really just like us is what we should be asking, right?

DAVID MUIR: What do you mean?

ELOISE MILLER: I mean, David, are they really people in the biblical sense?

DAVID MUIR: Biblical sense?

ELOISE MILLER: Think about it, David. God didn't make them, science did. They're not really like us, are they? They're not my kind. Are they your kind?

DAVID MUIR: That doesn't make sense.

ELOISE MILLER: Oh, it makes sense to most Americans, believe me. Most Americans agree with me—and the president—on this.

DAVID MUIR: But some members of the reanimation
                     community have done quite well integrat-
                     ing into our society, including winning
                     elected office . . .

ELOISE MILLER: Well . . .

DAVID MUIR: And one just pitched a no-hitter for the
                     Dodgers in yesterday's playoff . . .

ELOISE MILLER: But the exception proves the rule, right?
                     And we did just fine in both politics and
                     baseball before stitchers . . .

DAVID MUIR: But that's not the point . . .

ELOISE MILLER: No, that's exactly the point. Even the
                     so-called good stitchers are still taking
                     jobs away from real Americans.

DAVID MUIR: Unfortunately, we'll need to end it there.
                     Thank you, Secretary Miller, for spending
                     time with us.

ELOISE MILLER: My pleasure, David. My pleasure.

DAVID MUIR: Any final words?

ELOISE MILLER: Yes. Only one party can make America
                     safe again.

Chapter Ten

FAUSTINA AND THE MAN stood side by side on Leonard's doorstep, each staring straight ahead. Faustina held a bottle of pinot grigio. The man admired Leonard's door. He wondered who chose the bright red paint, Leonard or his husband. Perhaps the prior owners did. Or maybe the realtor, who wanted to give a pop of color in contrast to the subdued off-white paint chosen for the rest of the house. Yes, that must be it. The man saw that on HGTV. It's amazing how little tricks like that can work. The man suddenly realized that raucous laughter emanated from behind the red door.

"Sounds like someone is having fun," said Faustina.

"Yes," said the man.

"I suppose one of us should ring the doorbell."

"Yes."

They stood in silence without moving.

"I will introduce you as my friend," said Faustina.

"That would be an accurate statement," said the man.

Faustina looked at the man, who kept his eyes on Leonard's red door. She sighed, turned toward the door, and rang the doorbell. A neighbor's dog barked. They could hear someone yelling, "I'll get it!" After a few seconds, the door opened and the party's sounds spilled out.

"Faustina!" said Leonard, who held a boy with both arms. The boy buried his face into Leonard's chest. "Forgive Diego. He just woke up from a nap."

"He's so big!" said Faustina as she leaned in to give Leonard—and by default, his son—a hug.

"I know! I won't be able to carry him soon!"

Faustina pulled back and held up the bottle of pinot grigio so that Leonard could see the label.

"Oh, my favorite," said Leonard. He turned to the man. "And this is…?"

Faustina laughed. She introduced the man as her "good friend."

"Any good friend of Faustina's is a good friend of mine," said Leonard. "Excuse me if I don't shake hands, but as you can see, they are a bit busy right now."

The man nodded, smiled, and said, "Hello."

"Come on in," said Leonard as he moved to the side. "Plenty of food and drink just waiting for you. Hubby is behind the bar, per usual. Go say hi and put in your order."

"Your wish is my command," said Faustina.

The house undulated with people of all ages who laughed, chatted, ate, and drank. Faustina dutifully introduced the man to her law firm team members, their significant others, and a few children of various sizes and energy levels. All the while, Faustina kept an eye on the bar at the far end of the living room, where Leonard's husband took his role as bartender quite seriously.

"Almost there," whispered Faustina into the man's right ear.

The man nodded and appreciated Faustina's focus. After a few more introductions to various partygoers, they arrived at their destination.

"¡Hola, mi vida!" said Faustina.

"¡Hola, mi amor!" said Alejandro. "You look beautiful!"

"Not too loud, or else your hubby might hear."

"No te preocupes. He loves you too."

"Maybe I should marry the both of you and live happily ever after."

"Perfecto."

"And I wouldn't need to have a baby and ruin this hot body. Diego is all I need for a kid."

Alejandro laughed and then offered a welcoming smile to the man. "I'm Alejandro Venegas, Leonard's husband."

"Where are my manners?" said Faustina and introduced the man to Alejandro.

"Mucho gusto," said Alejandro.

"Mucho gusto," said the man.

"And how do you know each other?" said Alejandro.

"He is my very good friend," said Faustina.

The man turned to Faustina. "I thought I was just your good friend," he said.

Faustina laughed. "Yes, let me correct the record: he is my good friend, not my very good friend."

"I remember you," said Alejandro as he chuckled. "You attended the Yosemite environmental law conference."

"Yes," said the man, "I did."

"And here is a lovely bottle of pinot grigio to help restock your bar," said Faustina as she handed the wine to Alejandro, who examined the label with appreciation. He then set it aside with the other bottles of wine.

"What can I get for you two?" said Alejandro as he gestured toward the many bottles of alcohol arrayed before him. "I assume you will want a cocktail first, and then move to wine when you fill a plate with the wonderful food Leonard has been cooking all day."

"I want to experiment and try an old-timey drink," said Faustina.

"¡Qué interesante!" said Alejandro.

"I will have a Manhattan," said Faustina. "I watched *Some Like It Hot* for like the billionth time last week and that was the preferred drink of the lady band members."

"Old-timey is right, but a delicious choice and great movie too." Alejandro picked a glass from beneath the bar, set it down, and looked up at the man. "And are you having the same, or do you have a different movie drink in mind?"

The man thought about the movies he had watched since his reanimation three years ago. A coworker at his first law firm job ranked all of the James Bond films in order of quality based on this coworker's own private algorithm, which included factors such as the number of car crashes, beautiful women, drinks consumed, people shot, people tortured, the quality of the opening sequence song, and other key elements of Bond films. So the man promised his coworker to watch each one, which he did over the course of several months. He tried to remember what drinks 007 had in each movie. There were so many. The man thought for a moment.

"Rum Collins, please," the man finally said.

"Oh, interesting," said Alejandro. "Which film is that from?"

"*Thunderball*."

"Not my favorite Bond film, but a good drink."

Faustina looked at the man and let out a small laugh. "I didn't know you were a James Bond fan."

"See what you learn at parties," said Alejandro as he mixed the drinks.

"I have seen all of the Bond films once," said the man thoughtfully. "I don't know if that makes me a fan, but maybe it does. I never really thought about it."

Alejandro carefully set the finished drinks before Faustina and the man. "Drink up," he said. "Time to catch up with everyone else."

They grabbed their drinks. Faustina held hers out to clink with the man's glass. The man simply held his glass and looked at Faustina's glass suspended before him. He then realized what he needed to do, so he clinked his glass to hers. They each took a drink.

"Oh God, that is good," said Faustina.

"Gracias," said Alejandro. "And yours?"

The man nodded. "Yes, I like mine."

"Good! I have done my job to save thirsty souls! I am the Mother Teresa of cocktails. I am on my way to becoming a saint."

"Isn't death the first step to becoming a saint?" said the man.

Alejandro laughed. "So maybe I can skip that step for now."

"I have a question about your son," said the man.

Faustina's head jerked back just a bit, and she looked at the man.

"Yes?" said Alejandro. "What about Diego?"

"He looks like you, not Leonard."

"True. Is that a question?"

"No," said the man. "What I mean is, where did Diego come from?"

Alejandro smiled. "Oh, I see what you're getting at."

"Please forgive him," said Faustina. "He's very plainspoken."

"I do not mind at all," said Alejandro. "I prefer honesty."

A wobbly woman came up to the bar and held up an empty wineglass. Alejandro dutifully refilled it without missing a beat. The woman tried to curtsy but lost her balance and almost fell. She recovered, nodded, and wobbled off.

"My sperm and one surrogate," said Alejandro. "Leonard and I both supplied our own samples and let chance decide whose sperm would reach the egg first. IVF clinics wouldn't do that in years past. The most they'd do was use the two guys' sperm to fertilize multiple eggs so that it was still one egg being fertilized by one donor. But things have loosened up—regulation-wise."

"You mean with the drop in our country's birthrate?" said the man.

"Bingo!" said Alejandro. "All kinds of regulations have loosened up."

Faustina coughed a little and shot a look at Alejandro.

"Anyhoo," said Alejandro, "we found a clinic that would mix our sperm so that we'd leave it to chance as to who would be the biological father. Mine were clearly the faster swimmers. Well, at least one was."

Faustina almost spat out a mouthful of Manhattan as she stifled a laugh.

"Now, there have been remarkable breakthroughs with three-person IVF, where the one donor egg can be modified by two donor sperm—I don't know all of the exact terminology— but you get what I mean. But Leonard and I didn't want to go down that route. Too controversial, too sci-fi, you know what I mean?"

"Sci-fi?" said the man.

"You know, kind of too close to *Gattaca*."

"*Gattaca*?" said the man.

"The movie," said Faustina.

"Anyway," said Alejandro, "we wanted to leave a little to chance and not get too deep into genetic engineering."

"So," said the man, "if Leonard's sperm had been faster, Diego would have been darker?"

"¡Dios mío! You are plainspoken!" said Alejandro. "But yes, that likely would have been the case. Either way, we are blessed."

"Yes," said the man. "I agree. Either way, you two are blessed. You are lucky to have Diego."

Alejandro turned to Faustina and winked. Faustina shook her head and took a long drink of her Manhattan.

"Go mingle," said Alejandro. "And try some of the stuffed mushrooms. They are Leonard's masterpiece."

"Oh, I love his stuffed mushrooms!" said Faustina.

"But don't ruin your dinner," said Alejandro. "Leonard's tri-tip is manna from heaven."

"I know why you married him," said Faustina.

"He is a Renaissance man," said Alejandro. "A brilliant lawyer, an even better cook. Plus he ain't bad to look at."

Faustina raised her glass in agreement.

"Yes, I agree," said the man. "Leonard is very handsome."

Alejandro and Faustina looked at each other and then broke out in laughter simultaneously.

"I think I am beginning to appreciate this man's plainspoken manner," said Alejandro. "It's refreshing."

"It is that," said Faustina. "Refreshing is the perfect way to put it."

"Faustina!"

Faustina turned to where the voice came from. Across the room, on a couch, sat Grace and Brandon. Grace waved frantically at Faustina.

"Who is that?" said the man.

"My other law partner."

"Why is she smiling so much and waving like that?"

"She's dying to meet you, that's why."

"Oh."

Faustina took a long drink. "Okay, I'm ready for the lion's den."

"That's from the Bible," said the man.

"You are an educated man. Let's go."

"Have fun," said Alejandro. "And nice to meet you."

"Nice to meet you," said the man.

Faustina grabbed the man's arm and put it around her waist. "Fuck it. Let's give her a show," she said as she pulled the man along. "You only live twice."

"Number six," said the man.

"What?"

"On my old coworker's list of best Bond films."

"Well, let's make it number one," said Faustina. "Let's say hi to Grace and her hubby."

"I HAD A NICE time tonight," said Faustina. She rested her head on the man's bare chest as they lay in his bed under a rumpled sheet. A lamp in the far corner of the room gave off a soft amber glow.

"I am glad I met your friends," said the man.

They were silent for three minutes before Faustina broke the silence: "What was all that about Diego's skin color?"

"I wanted to understand," said the man as he stared up at the ceiling.

"Understand what?"

"How Diego came to be."

"Oh," said Faustina. "I guess I just took it for granted since I've known Leonard and Alejandro for so long. They actually came to me when they first started looking for a surrogate. They thought that I might want to do it, but it was too much of a commitment."

"Commitment?"

"Even though they would have adopted the child to make it legal, if I carried that baby in me for nine months, I would have had, you know, feelings."

"Feelings?"

"Motherly feelings. I think it's inevitable, don't you?"

"I don't know."

"I suspect most men would not know or even understand the concern," said Faustina.

The man thought about this. He did not have another question.

"But no matter," said Faustina. "Like I said, I had a nice time tonight."

"Thank you," said the man.

"Oh, you're taking all the credit for my good time?"

"No, that's not what I was thanking you for."

"Oh."

"Thank you for inviting me to the party."

"Actually, if you think about it, my mother invited you," said Faustina. "So what choice did I have?"

The man let out a little laugh.

"Oh, so you find me funny?"

The man nodded.

"Happy to entertain you," said Faustina.

"Well," said the man, "it is a funny statement because, in the end, you always have a choice. So you could have told your mother that you were not ready to have your coworkers meet me. And I know you are not shy about saying how you feel. That much I know."

"Well, either way, I actually had a good time," said Faustina. "It wasn't as weird as I thought it would be."

The man held Faustina. After a few minutes, he could hear her snore softly. The man smiled and stared at the ceiling. Within a few more minutes, the man fell asleep, his soft snores falling into sync with hers.

Chapter Eleven

THE MAN FELL INTO his dream, the same dream he had each night since his reanimation. In the dream, faces—some familiar, some not—flickered and ebbed into view. Lips moved, words muttered, but the man could not discern their meaning. And then silence. Not a sound to be heard. Suddenly, the amorphous surroundings transformed into a beach, and the man found himself standing at the edge of the water. He looked down and saw that he carried a body draped in a white shroud. A voice commanded the man to step into a small boat that floated in the water before him. "What should I do with this body?" the man asked the disembodied voice.

"Toss it into the boat," the voice answered. And the man did what he was told. He settled in near the body and the boat started to move forward of its own volition, the rippling water making a strange whispering sound.

As the boat steadily moved across what appeared to be an endless lake, the man forgot about the body that rested at his feet. His stomach rumbled and he allowed his mind to drift to imagined sumptuous meals that he had no memory of ever consuming before. How did he know what these foods tasted like? The boat finally reached the other side of the lake. The man lifted the shrouded body and put it on his back. He stepped out of the boat and onto the warm sand. The man grew angry with himself because he had forgotten to ask the disembodied voice for further direction. But no matter. He would trudge forward. As he did, the man noticed that the terrain changed. Strange trees and plants sprouted from what was now a rocky, craggy ground. The man marched a very long time, and the shrouded body grew heavier with each step, his bare feet getting cut by the sharp, rocky ground. The man eventually realized that the terrain had grown more fantastical with each step. Indeed, the shapes he saw seemed to become something more than terrain, something akin to a language. Not merely a language but a hieroglyph, ancient and mysterious, that spoke only to him. Without much effort, he deciphered the message. The man now knew what he needed to do.

The man, armed with knowledge, finally reached the place where he could allow himself to put the shrouded body down so that he could rest and gather his wits. He looked up and saw a large boulder shaped like a hand holding a ripe fig. The boulder balanced upon a pedestal of rock that jutted up from the sand. With a strength he did not possess while awake, the man lifted the shrouded body and inserted it between the boulder and the rock. When he had completed this task, the man offered up a simple benediction: "Sleep, sleep."

After a few moments of silence, the man started his long trek back to the boat. He walked through the strange, craggy terrain, which gave way to the gentle sand that he had first encountered.

The sun warmed his body and the gentle sand seeped through his toes with each step. But his serenity was dashed when a group of dark figures without faces surrounded him. The man tried to scream but couldn't open his mouth. These dark figures pulled at the man's arms—first his left, then his right—and bit his face and body as they snarled like rabid dogs. This torture went on and on and on. Finally, the dark figures dropped the man onto the ground and lurched away, muttering obscene sounds that were not quite words. The man lay bruised and bleeding, but in time he gathered himself up and stood. The man felt his body and confirmed that he was intact. And slowly he resumed his journey, limping in pain with each step.

The man made it to the boat, which seemed to be waiting for him. He got in, sat down, and closed his eyes. The man could feel the boat move, sliding slowly across the vast lake in the direction from where he had come. He eventually felt a presence near the boat, floating out before him in the water. The man's eyes popped open and what he saw made him smile. A few yards from the boat's bow floated the dark figures that had accosted him previously. *There is justice*, thought the man. The boat slid by the bodies and the man grinned in satisfaction at the flotsam and jetsam that had been his tormentors.

In time the man's boat reached the shore. His bruises and lacerations had miraculously healed, and he felt fit and strong. He stepped out of the boat. The moment his left foot touched the sand, the man fell into darkness, fast and dizzying, deep, deep, deep into an abyss. Before the man hit the bottom, he awoke from his dream.

The man sat up. He breathed heavily, and a cold sheen of perspiration covered his body. The man looked upon Faustina, sleeping on her side facing him, curled into a ball like a cat, and snoring, face half buried in the man's pillow. The sheet had fallen to the floor, and the soft amber light of the corner lamp bathed Faustina's body in a gentle glow. The man softly touched Faustina's skin at her left shoulder and then at her hip. Perfectly joined, not a line of rippled scar tissue, simply beautiful brown skin running seamlessly along the contours of her limbs. His breathing slowed as he calmed from the delirium of the nightmare.

The man sighed, stood, and walked into the bathroom. He closed the door and turned on the light. He looked in the mirror and considered the differences between Faustina's body and his own. The man slowly ran his fingers across the scar tissue where his left hip and leg joined. A fairly good match of skin color and even in foot size. His own right foot takes a size-nine medium shoe, but the man could comfortably walk about wearing a nine and a half, the size of the foot on his new leg.

The man then ran his fingers along the scars where his left arm had been joined at the shoulder. His own right arm and shoulder were, of course, perfect together. But the left... the jarring line of color looked like a children's wooden jigsaw puzzle of the United States with each state a different color from its neighbor. Couldn't they have found skin that was closer in hue? The brown of his left shoulder stood out against the white of the arm. And his left hand was so much larger than his right. A shocking mismatch. Why? Was it some kind of cruel joke? Did the surgeons and nurses laugh and offer sniggering jibes about the man's patchwork body parts? How could anyone be so cruel as to deny him the modest gift of conformity, that inner peace that springs from ordinariness, an opportunity to simply be only himself and not contain many? He didn't seem to belong anywhere. Neither here nor there.

The man then reached up to examine his face—using his right hand—and traced the outlines of his eyebrows, nose, lips, chin. He turned his face left and then right. He wondered what he had originally looked like. The man sighed and closed his eyes for a moment. He then reached into his medicine cabinet and retrieved a plastic prescription bottle. The man examined it, opened the bottle, and poured the red, oblong pills out onto the counter. He carefully fingered each pill, counting them out. Thirty-one pills left. He sighed. The man cautiously picked up each pill and dropped it into the bottle, closed it, and put the bottle back in the medicine cabinet.

The man clicked off the bathroom lights and stood in complete darkness. Without light, he was nothing more than one person. He reached for the doorknob and carefully opened the door so that it would not emit a creak. The soft amber light of the bedroom slowly filled the bathroom. The man walked toward the bed and looked upon the slumbering Faustina. So beautiful! His head ached, and he sighed. The man turned and walked out of the bedroom to his study. He turned on the desk lamp and opened the bottom drawer of his filing cabinet. The man peered into the drawer, hesitated, then pulled out a battered cardboard box. He placed the box onto his desk, sat, and considered his next action.

The man jumped with a start when Faustina let out a loud cough followed by sounds of her stirring, limbs rearranging. He froze, waiting to see if she had awakened. After a few moments, she quieted, save for a soft snore. The man turned back to the box and lifted its lid. He smiled, reached in, and retrieved a children's picture book. He thumbed through the brittle, curled pages, and then closed it. On the cover was a business card attached with a paperclip. The card said:

Dr. Marco Prietto
Clerval Industries

Beneath the doctor's telephone number and address were the words *when you are ready,* written at the bottom in red pen. The man let those four words roll around in his mind. He smiled. And at that moment, the man finally understood what those words meant. He gingerly placed the book in the cardboard box, and returned the box to the drawer. The man clicked off the desk lamp and walked slowly to his bedroom. He slid the sheet back onto Faustina, who stirred just a bit but then fell still. The man silently opened a dresser drawer and retrieved his hoodie, sweatpants, jockstrap, and socks. He dressed, slipped on his running shoes, and looked upon Faustina one more time before leaving the bedroom.

Chapter Twelve

THE MAN CLOSED HIS apartment door and entered the cool evening. He stretched his legs and twirled his arms in three clockwise circles. The man took a deep breath, put on his hoodie, and then started on his nightly run, though it was much later than usual. In fact, it was almost two in the morning. He turned left on Hurlbut Street toward Pasadena Avenue and then turned left again. The man let his legs stretch out in long strides as his muscles slowly warmed up. He concentrated on his breathing. The man sensed the strength of his legs and arms as he ran, but something seemed off. He almost felt connected to each part of himself, but not quite. The man picked up speed as he ran along Pasadena Avenue.

CNN'S ANDERSON COOPER INTERVIEWS THE PRESIDENT

COOPER: Thank you for joining us this evening, President Cadwallader.

POTUS: My pleasure as always, Anderson.

COOPER: A new poll from CNN shows that your party has seen an uptick in the generic midterm numbers, now pulling ahead by about three percentage points but just within the margin of error.

POTUS: Slow but steady wins the race, Anderson. And I think those numbers show that our message is being heard by the American people.

COOPER: Your message being?

POTUS: Make America safe again!

COOPER: Right. But some would argue that the MASA movement is built on fear and offers no real solutions to rising inflation, climate change, the chronic lack of affordable housing, and somewhat lackluster job growth while you've been president, even though your party has enjoyed majorities in both houses.

POTUS: But the American people know that none of that means anything unless they are safe in their own homes, places of business, and schools. What's more real: Alarmist cries about alleged climate change and rising sea levels, or a family's fear of violence while simply walking in their own neighborhood in broad daylight? We have a real crisis, Anderson, and my party is offering solutions, while the other side only wants us to give another government handout or destroy our economy with environmental red tape. Real Americans know what the real threats are, and so do I. After all, it was my party that passed the anti-stitcher law without one vote from the other side.

COOPER: The, er, law that banned reanimation is a case in point. It seemed to be working—the reanimation industry, that is—before the ban, without many negative side effects for our economy and . . .

POTUS: I beg to differ, Anderson. There have been documented incidents of violence . . . shovings and the like.

COOPER: Well, those reports are a mixed bag and inconclusive, really, based on the somewhat spotty news coverage. Some reports indicate that the "shovings"—as you put it—were provoked and really incidents of self-defense. And in terms of violence and people feeling safe, there have been literally hundreds of mass shootings since you've been president, and none of those involved members of the reanimated community. Those were homegrown . . .

POTUS: But do we have to wait until the shov-
                        ings become shootings? And the other
                        side wants to de-arm regular Americans
                        so we won't be able to protect ourselves
                        once some of these stitchers decide to
                        graduate from shovings to assault rifles.

COOPER: There's no evidence that is going to
                        happen, and you've fought against any
                        kind of gun reform—even something
                        such as improved background checks,
                        which most Americans support, based
                        on the polling.

POTUS: There's no evidence that stitchers aren't
                        arming themselves right now as we
                        speak, in our own backyards across
                        America. No, I will not stand idly by
                        while the other party stands on critical
                        stitcher theory to protect the very enemy
                        of our way of life.

COOPER: I'm sorry, President Cadwallader, I don't
                        believe you can just make that kind of
                        argument without any sort of evidence.

POTUS: And on top of it, the stitcher industry was
                        rife with abuses, all quite documented,
                        you know that.

COOPER: Some documented abuses, as you put it.
                        Just a few stories about reanimation doc-
                        tors communicating with their subjects
                        after they were reintroduced into soci-
                        ety. But nothing particularly offensive
                        or dangerous.

POTUS: That's only if you consider social engi-
                neering a good thing, which I don't. We
                have to protect our own, that's what it
                comes down to.

COOPER: Such rhetoric could turn off the reani-
                mated vote, are you concerned about
                that? I mean, they vote in relatively high
                numbers and could tip a close election.

POTUS: Dead people voting . . .

COOPER: No, that's not what I said . . .

POTUS: That's how elections are stolen, Anderson!
                You've laid out my case for me.

COOPER: No, that's not what I meant . . .

POTUS: And should dead people vote? That's
                something we're going to look at if we
                keep both the House and Senate. The
                dead should not be allowed to enjoy our
                most precious of American rights, espe-
                cially to push a stitcher agenda. What's
                next? A stitcher who has two, three, or
                more donors to their body who can vote
                once, twice, three times? We've got to
                true our elections, and keeping stitchers
                out of the voting booth is how we start
                to clean things up. If we don't, we're
                screwed . . . pardon my French.

COOPER: But when people signed their donor
                cards to allow themselves to be reani-
                mated, they were promised all the rights
                they had previously. If you try to change
                that, you will be violating their vested

	rights. And as you know, there's a fair amount of case law on the protection of a person's vested rights. Lawsuits will be filed, no doubt.
POTUS:	And that's why we need litigation reform to stop frivolous lawsuits that only line the pockets of trial attorneys. And that's also why I need a Senate that will continue to confirm my Supreme Court nominees, should a vacancy happen in the near future. Too much is at stake in this election.
COOPER:	I think that's one thing we can agree on. Thank you, President Cadwallader. We'll have to stop here; we are out of time.
POTUS:	Thank you, Anderson. Not only do you ask great questions, but you look wonderful too. You seem to get younger every day.
COOPER:	Er, thank you? In any event, good night, and we'll be watching how these midterm elections shake out.
POTUS:	Good night, Anderson, and God bless the real America.

Chapter Thirteen

THE MAN SLOWLY DRAGGED a knife through the stack of six corn tortillas while Faustina drizzled olive oil into the hot skillet, which reacted by emitting a sizzle and pop. Faustina turned to the man and watched as he meticulously lifted the knife and began the process again.

"Such a perfectionist," said Faustina.

"You said you liked them to be in triangles," said the man as he concentrated on his task. "But that is actually impossible unless I trim away the rounded ends, and you told me not to do that. So I am trying to make them as close to triangles as I can, even if they have rounded bottoms."

"I did indeed. Some people actually just tear the tortillas up by hand, no neat edges, just raggedness all around. In the end, chilaquiles do not require perfection."

The man looked up. "What do they require?"

"Just the right amount of crispiness—in my book, at least—and since these are chilaquiles rojos, the sauce must be made fresh from tomatoes, a little onion, jalapeños, garlic, and a bit of chicken broth. But there are probably a million different recipes out there. The key is to follow your family's tradition, especially if you're going to feed your relatives, because believe me, family can be pretty harsh critics when it comes to culinary traditions. One divergence from a family recipe, and you'll never hear the end of it! It will become that story told each Christmas about how so-and-so screwed up the posole or lengua or enchiladas or arroz or chilaquiles. I mean, I still haven't told my mother that I use olive oil instead of her trusty Wesson, though I think she suspects. In any event, it's safer to keep critics mollified by sticking with family tradition as much as possible."

"Yes, that makes sense," said the man as he returned to cutting the tortillas. "I could see how you'd want to avoid that."

"And of course, with chilaquiles, you need to top it with queso fresco, though some like cotija, but that makes the chilaquiles too salty for my taste. On top of all that is an over easy egg, though I am quite content to go without. But again, I need to be careful about getting too creative or else I won't hear the end of it!"

The man ran the knife through the tortillas one more time, examined his handiwork, smiled, and then dropped the pieces into a large orange bowl that held the three previous batches of cut tortillas.

"Perfecto," said Faustina as she lifted the bowl and examined the man's tortilla-cutting artistry. "You get an A-plus for neatness. Not only are you guapo but you are a sous chef in the making." She then reached into the bowl, plucked out one tortilla triangle, and dropped it into the skillet. It sizzled and popped.

"Testing the oil?" said the man.

"Precisely!"

"I like the sound it makes."

"It is pretty satisfying, isn't it? Simple pleasures."

"Is it ready?"

"Yes, it's ready," said Faustina as she slowly dropped handfuls of tortilla triangles into the skillet, the sizzling and popping growing in volume as the mound grew.

As Faustina continued to cook, the man watched her efficient movements in an attempt to etch upon his memory this moment. He liked her kitchen better than his own. It gleamed and possessed a layout that perfectly matched Faustina's culinary requirements. The man's kitchen, on the other hand, seemed ill-conceived, with an island that was too large for such a small room. And he couldn't open the island's cabinets at the same time the oven door was open or else there'd be a collision of wood and metal. The only true benefit of his kitchen was that all of the large appliances had been updated when the apartment complex underwent renovations before he had moved in. But in the end, he should not be surprised by the discrepancy between their respective living spaces. Faustina owned a mid-century modern, 2,200-square-foot house, while the man rented an apartment half that size. The man was not bitter about this difference; he merely acknowledged Faustina's financial security, which came with being a named partner in a successful law firm. Besides, the man had now been spending time at Faustina's house rather than Faustina staying at his, which had been her desire during the first two weeks of their relationship—if that's the appropriate term. Now, four weeks into dating, Faustina preferred having the man stay at her home a few nights a week; the other nights she kept to herself, or perhaps she would stay over at the man's apartment every so often. It was simply more convenient for her, she had said. But the man assumed it was something else—he didn't know what—though he had no quarrel with the arrangement. He was approaching a feeling that he had not had before, a feeling of contentment, security, peace. And the man was more than willing to follow Faustina's lead when it came to their budding relationship. In the end, he trusted her to offer the most efficient and practical logistical solutions for everything from making chilaquiles to the conduct of their dating life.

"Could you set the table?" said Faustina as she continued to add ingredients to the skillet, causing a little sizzle with each new item. "Mom and Saul will be here soon."

"Yes," said the man as he opened a drawer and withdrew forks, knives, and spoons.

"And use the cloth napkins, please. They are in that cabinet over there."

"Yes."

"And if you could put the fruit salad out along with the orange juice, that would be perfect. I can start the coffee in a sec."

"Yes, I can do that," said the man as he breathed in the aroma of the chilaquiles-in-progress. "It smells good."

Faustina turned to look at the man. "I can teach you," she smiled, then turned back to cooking. "You know what they say."

"What do they say?"

"If you give a man a fish, you have fed him for a day, but…"

The man waited for Faustina to finish her sentence. After a few moments, the man said, "But what?"

Faustina turned to the man. "You really haven't heard this one before?"

"No, I don't think so. It depends on what else you say before I know whether I've heard it before."

"But if you teach him to fish, you have fed him for a lifetime."

The man smiled. "That's new to me. And I like it. It makes sense."

"I have a million of them!"

"Oh, good."

"You're an easy audience."

The doorbell rang.

"Oh!" said Faustina. "They're here a bit early. I'm still wrestling with the chilaquiles. Please get the door, if you don't mind."

"Sure."

The man looked at the table he had just set. It appeared balanced, just right. He nodded to himself, rapped on the table three times, and strolled to the foyer as the doorbell rang again. The man opened the door and stood back.

"There you are!" said Saul. "I was getting worried that we had the wrong day. I'm having more than my fair share of senior moments!"

"You have the right day," said the man.

Verónica reached up to hug the man. He hugged back and smiled. Saul shook the man's hand and handed him a bottle of prosecco.

"Something to spike the orange juice with," winked Saul. "It will improve the appetite and loosen our tongues."

"The chilaquiles smell good," said Verónica as she slowly walked into the kitchen. "Almost as good as mine!"

"¡Ay!" said Faustina as she wiped her hands on a small towel before hugging her mother. "I was taught by the best. But Pop's chilaquiles were pretty good too."

"Who do you think taught your father?" Verónica laughed.

"Yes, Mamá, your recipe is the best, and you are a wonderful teacher," said Faustina.

"Por supuesto," said Verónica. "My beautiful daughter does not lie."

"She does not," said the man. "She does not."

"SO THERE I WAS, curled up next to Verónica—fully clothed on top of the blanket, mind you, except for my shoes—on that narrow hospital bed trying to nap just a little, and in walks the nurse."

"I was so embarrassed!" said Verónica.

Faustina lifted the last forkful of chilaquiles to her mouth and said, "What happened?"

Saul took a sip of his orange juice and prosecco. "Well, the nurse says, 'Oh, I don't think you should be in bed with her,' and I said…"

"No, don't tell this!" said Verónica as she covered her face with her hands. "This is so embarrassing!"

"And I said," continued Saul, "in a perfectly normal voice: 'Don't worry, I bought her dinner first!'"

Saul let out a guffaw that shook the dining room. Faustina couldn't help but join in with a snorted laugh. Verónica shook her head, smiling but glowing a bright red. The man smiled, impressed with Saul's ability to think so fast in such a strange, embarrassing situation.

When the laughter subsided, Verónica turned to Faustina and said, "You know, your father had the same sense of humor."

Faustina sighed. "Yep, Pop would have made the same joke, or maybe a little dirtier."

Saul chuckled. "I'm sure I would have liked Agustín."

The dining room fell into silence, everyone with their own private thoughts.

"May I get anything else for anyone?" asked the man as he stood.

"So polite," said Verónica. "No gracias. I am so full!"

"I can't fit another thing in my very happy stomach," said Saul.

"A little more coffee for me," said Faustina.

The man walked to the kitchen and froze to gather his composure. He had been trying to stay calm since the beginning of brunch. The man thought he had seen the face of a woman he didn't recognize when he had closed his eyes after taking that first mouthful of chilaquiles. This had happened before, maybe a dozen times that he could remember. It was triggered by anything from the taste of particular foods to hearing certain phrases or bits of music. He shook his head and allowed his composure to return just enough to keep functioning. The man retrieved the coffeepot, walked back to the dining room, refilled Faustina's cup, then returned the coffeepot to the kitchen. The man came back to the dining room, sat, reached for the half-and-half, poured some into Faustina's cup, stirred it, and settled back into his chair.

"Such service!" said Saul. "A girl could get used to that."

It was Faustina's turn to blush. "Anyhoo…"

The conversation paused for a moment, then started up again, full tilt, with Verónica noting how Agustín was a thoughtful husband but not very good in the kitchen.

"Before I taught him a few recipes, his sole idea of cooking was to take whatever leftovers he could scrounge up and mix it with eggs in an unusual scramble," said Verónica. "And I mean anything. ¡Ay! He'd mix my delicious arroz and make a Mexican rice omelet!"

"And don't forget his chopped, fried Oscar Meyer hot dogs and eggs," laughed Faustina.

"Huevos con weenies!" said Verónica.

"That concoction, with steaming corn tortillas, made a well-balanced, perfect meal for the family as far as Pop was concerned," said Faustina. "Pop always said: You need a lot of protein to keep your brain working at full capacity!"

"I don't know if I've had huevos con weenies before," said the man.

"Oh, you must have," said Faustina. "It's a Mexican classic. Pop didn't invent it, but he certainly acted like he did."

Saul grinned and nodded. "I wish I knew Agustín."

"And I wish I could have met your Rachel," said Verónica.

"You two would have liked each other," said Saul.

"Someday we will all be together," offered Verónica.

Saul laughed. "I wish I had your faith on that point."

"Ni modo," said Verónica, offering a sweet, sad smile to Saul. "We'll eventually know what there is after we are called back. All I know is that life can be filled with surprises."

"One door closes, another opens," agreed Saul, returning the smile.

"How did you two meet?" said the man.

"Oh," said Faustina, "this is a strange story."

"Not so strange," said Verónica. "Mija, you know what I always say…"

"I know, I know: 'Todo es parte del plan de Dios.'"

"I wish I could get a copy of this plan!" laughed Saul.

"¡Ay!" said Verónica as she gently patted Saul's arm. "Some things you shouldn't joke about. If God wanted us to know his plan, he'd publish it in the newspaper. We have to have faith that there is a plan."

"Anyhow," said Saul, "we met at Forest Lawn a little more than a year ago."

"The cemetery?" said the man.

"The very same," said Saul. "We had just finished the unveiling of my Rachel's headstone."

"Unveiling?" said the man.

"It's a Jewish ceremony," said Saul. "Within the first year after the passing of a loved one, we get together at the gravesite for a ceremony where we say Kaddish—the mourner's prayer—and we remove a veil from the tombstone. Sort of like a formal dedication. Rachel and I never could have any kids, so it was just me, my brother, and his wife—their twin girls were off at college in Massachusetts—so it was a small group. We didn't even have a rabbi because, well, we sort of stopped going to shul years ago. So my brother agreed to lead us in the ceremony. He's a dentist but was always more religious, so he was happy to oblige. He did a beautiful job. He'll always have another gig to fall back on if he gets tired of dentistry."

Verónica gently squeezed Saul's arm. Saul looked down and blinked, lost in thought.

"And how did you meet Faustina's mother?" said the man.

"Well, after the unveiling," said Saul, "my brother and sister-in-law had to catch a plane, so I decided to walk around a bit and look at the other headstones and plaques. The grounds are actually quite beautiful, very peaceful, which I suppose makes sense. All kinds of religions represented in the designs. Kind of lovely to see everyone getting along, side by side like that, even though they're dead, right? You can get to thinking about a lot of things as you look around a cemetery."

"Like what?" said the man.

"Well, for one thing, it's amazing how many folks passed away at a young age in their twenties and thirties," said Saul.

"Some of the headstones were for children and babies too. So sad."

"Ay," added Verónica with a mournful shake of her head.

"You're going to make me cry," said Faustina.

"So after looking at various headstones," said Saul, "I go up this walkway and end up at one of the crypts that had dozens of plaques going up maybe fifteen feet or more. I started to wander, reading a plaque here and there, and then I saw this lovely woman struggling with one of those poles they let you use to put flowers at the higher plaques."

"That was me," smiled Verónica. "Your father had been gone two years already, and I wanted him to know that I still remembered him. I like to visit him and tell him how things are going here, and that he is missed. I also thank him for everything he gave us."

"That's beautiful, my love," said Saul. "So, where was I? Oh yeah. I trot up to this lovely woman and offer to help. She looked at me, a little startled, but handed the pole to me without a word, offering the sweetest, most beautiful smile. I quickly but carefully set the flowers in the little vase holder they have near each memorial plaque. She thanked me profusely and gave me more of that beautiful smile. And the rest, as they say, is history."

"Yes, you all have so much history," said the man. "With each other and before."

Faustina, Verónica, and Saul looked at the man.

"Why, yes," ventured Faustina, "I guess we do have that."

Saul smiled, then said, "Hey, I got this great email from my brother with some new jokes. He always sends me a new list."

"Oh no," said Verónica. "I've heard them already. Some are not so funny."

"Let them decide!" said Saul, undeterred.

"Hit me," said Faustina. "I could use a good joke."

"Okay, a synagogue has a mouse problem. The place is crawling with mice, lousy with mice! Thousands of them everywhere, coming in and out of every crevice and corner. Oy! The custodian tries traps, baits, cats, everything. Nothing works. Finally he goes to the rabbi and explains the problem, because the rabbi is a very wise man who seems to have answers for every question, big or small. 'I have the solution,' the rabbi says after thinking for a moment. 'Well, what is it?' says the custodian. 'It's a foolproof plan,' the rabbi says, smiling. 'I'm listening,' says the custodian. The rabbi finally answers, 'I'll give them all Bar Mitzvahs—we'll never see them again!'"

Saul punctuated the punchline with a guffaw. Verónica shrugged. Faustina nodded, smiled, chuckled, and said, "That's pretty good."

"I don't get it," said Verónica.

"I tried to explain it, honey," said Saul.

"Let me try," said Faustina. "Substitute 'Bar Mitzvahs' with 'confirmations.'"

Verónica thought. After a few seconds, a smile appeared, and then a chuckle escaped.

"Bingo!" said Saul. "That's how I should have explained it."

"That's a pretty funny joke," said Verónica. "Okay, try another!"

Saul rubbed his hands together. "Okay, let me think…"

"Tell a political one," said Faustina. "The election is around the corner, and I've been filling out my absentee ballot. Such craziness this year! You must have a political joke."

"Oh, he has a lot of those," said Verónica.

As Saul began another joke, this time much longer, the man

leaned back and absorbed the scene. He smiled. *This is what a family looks and sounds like,* he thought. *Histories and stories and jokes and love and laughter.* And as these thoughts rolled about in his mind, the man was convinced more than ever of what he needed to do.

Chapter Fourteen

AFTER THE BRUNCH, FAUSTINA sent the man on his way
because she needed to prepare for a deposition in San Francisco
the next day. It would be a one-day trip, no more. The man
kissed Faustina and wished her luck. When he got back to his
apartment, he walked straight to his study. He turned on the
desk lamp and opened the bottom drawer of his filing cabinet.
The man pulled out the battered cardboard box, placed it on
his desk, lifted its lid, took out the children's picture book, and
sat in his desk chair. He removed the business card that was
clipped to the book's cover, laid it carefully to one side of the
desk, and tapped it three times. The man opened the book. He
smiled, sighed, and read the title aloud: *"The Story of Fernando."*
He turned to the first page and started to read the picture book
to himself:

*This is the story of how Fernando became my very best friend.
He possesses every quality one could ask for in a friend. He knows his
manners, he speaks many languages—like Spanish and English—and*

he could only be described as most handsome. Fernando's hair is shiny, like a moist winter night, and his eyes sparkle with great intelligence and wit.

Fernando has only one drawback. When Fernando gets caught in the rain he, well, how can I put this delicately? When he gets wet, Fernando stinks. Not just a little stink. But a big stink.

Why, do you ask, does he stink when he gets wet? Well, that's a really good question. You see, Fernando is a furry animal. From the very first day he was born in the hills of the San Fernando Valley, he was a member of the weasel family. Specifically, Fernando is a ferret. In Spanish, un hurón.

Some of you might be wriggling up your noses and shaking your heads now that you know that Fernando is a ferret. And some of you may also know that it is illegal to own a ferret as a pet in California (and Hawaii, too, for that matter). Granted, ferrets don't have the kind of reputation enjoyed by cute puppies and cuddly kittens. But they are beautiful creatures. Most ferrets have lustrous cream-colored coats with dark tips on their feet and tails and a dusky mask of fur around their eyes. But none of this is really important, because I can't own pets. You see, I'm an insect known as a beetle. My name is Betty. Glad to make your acquaintance.

My story begins a year before I actually met Fernando. That's when Fernando was born in the hills of the San Fernando Valley, in that large city known as Los Angeles, in the state of California. The night Fernando came into this world could only be described as warm and treacherous because of the hot winds that blew hard and relentlessly that night. Scientists call them the Santa Ana winds, but a lot of people simplify by calling them santanas. But the winds are also called devil winds because they are so hot, and strange things can happen when they blow through the San Fernando Valley.

The night Fernando was born, the moon shone bright and hard on the trees, shrubs, and hills where Fernando's parents, Isabel and Miguel, tried to keep their minds off the heat. Crickets were too hot to chirp, and even the moths could do nothing more than lounge about and think about cooler nights.

"And what shall we name him?" asked Isabel.

"Hmm," thought Miguel. "Didn't we say that we would try to name one of our males after my grandfather?"

"Yes, we did," said Isabel.

"Then it's decided, isn't it?"

Isabel looked down at her new baby. "Yes, it's decided. We will call him Fernando."

Just then, Fernando let out a little yelp.

"Ha!" laughed Miguel. "He already knows his name!"

"Yes, he does," said Isabel. "He's our little Fernando."

Isabel and Miguel were very fine parents, as are most ferrets. And because they were who they were, they taught little Fernando everything a young ferret should learn. In other words, Isabel and Miguel taught Fernando how to hunt. Lessons started in earnest just after Fernando's first birthday. At first Fernando thought that the whole thing was just another game. He laughed and giggled as his father showed him how to wriggle and point his nose to pick up a scent.

"All ferrets must first learn to aim their noses into the wind to pick up a scent," said Miguel to his son.

With that, Miguel lifted his elegant nose, closed his eyes, and sniffed into the warm summer breeze. Fernando kept his sharp eyes trained on his father. Fernando's little nostrils flared as he concentrated on the lesson. Though Miguel kept his eyes shut, he could sense that Fernando was quietly observing his every move.

"What is the magic word that every ferret must remember?" asked Miguel as he wriggled his nose back and forth.

Fernando thought for a moment. "Please?"

"No."

"Thank you?"

"No," said Miguel. "Besides, that's two words."

"Oh," said Fernando.

"I'm talking about hunting now," said Miguel. "Not manners."

"Yes, Papá," said Fernando, feeling a bit embarrassed. Indeed, if ferrets could blush, Fernando would have been a bright shade of crimson right then.

Miguel, becoming a bit impatient, said, "The magic word is 'patience.'"

"Oh yes!" Fernando smiled with his tiny but sharp teeth. "Patience!"

"Do not forget that!" said Miguel as he lifted his nose back up into the breeze. Just then, I crawled by Fernando's left paw.

"Oh, hello," said Fernando to me.

I jumped not because I was afraid of Fernando but because I couldn't believe that a ferret could speak such perfect beetle.

"Why, hello to you," I said once I recovered from my surprise. "You speak beetle very well."

"Oh, thank you," said Fernando, putting his nose closer to me. "I like speaking different languages. I guess I have what's called a gift."

"It is truly a gift," I said.

"Thank you," said Fernando.

Miguel suddenly realized that he had lost the attention of his student. He opened his left eye and saw Fernando chattering away to the ground.

"Fernando, what are you doing making such odd noises to the dirt?" asked Miguel as he opened his other eye and lowered his snout.

"Talking to a beetle, Papá."

Miguel shook his head in disbelief. "Why would you do a thing like that?"

"Well, Papá, I like to talk to different creatures," smiled Fernando. "They're interesting."

Fernando then looked back at me. "By the way, what is your name?"

"Betty," I said.

Fernando's father grew impatient. "Interesting?" asked Miguel. "What can be interesting about a bug?"

"That's the thing," answered Fernando. "A beetle is different from a fly, a ladybug, a gnat, a butterfly, a caterpillar, a moth, or a bee."

"All right, Fernando, all right!" Miguel laughed. "I think I understand what you mean. Now, go ahead and eat it and move on!"

At this I jumped. "What did he say?"

Fernando whispered to me: "Don't worry. I never eat anything that has introduced itself to me. When I give you a wink, jump into that little hole behind you."

Fernando's father said impatiently, "Well?"

Fernando looked up and said in a loud voice, "Yes, I'll eat him right away. He sure looks delicious!"

Even though I knew he was not going to eat me, this last comment made me a bit nervous. Then Fernando gave me a wink. As agreed, I jumped into the little hole so that Fernando's father couldn't see me. Fernando dipped his head, made a gulping sound, and then smacked his lips.

"Yum!" he said. "Delicious!"

"Good job!" Fernando's father said. "Now let's get moving."

Fernando gave me another wink and whispered, "See you later, Betty."

I whispered, "Yes, later!"

And that is how Fernando and I became friends. Friends can come in all shapes, sizes, and colors. Don't you agree? But this is not the end of my story. Oh no! Something else happened that I must tell you about.

Pretty soon Fernando's father, Miguel, figured that Fernando knew all there was for a ferret to know about hunting for food. So Miguel would let Fernando go out on his own to search for something good to eat. This is when Fernando and I would meet and play.

One day I was lolling around the nice, warm dirt waiting for Fernando. The wildflowers had recently bloomed into beautiful bursts of yellows, purples, and reds. A family of quail scurried about, and the fluffy white clouds blew across the brilliant blue sky. Suddenly, I heard Fernando calling me. He was speaking in perfect beetle. I looked up and saw him standing near a large pile of rocks.

"Fernando!" I said as loudly as I could. But he didn't hear me. Suddenly, the ground started to shake and rumble, and I thought to myself that some large animal must be stomping close by. Then I realized that this was no animal! It was an earthquake! Then I noticed that the pile of rocks above Fernando started to shift, just a bit. The earthquake had set the rocks in motion. They started to teeter and Fernando didn't notice what was happening!

"¡Temblor!" I yelled. This time Fernando heard me. He ran in my direction as the rocks came crashing down and landed where Fernando had been standing! Fernando ran even faster and eventually reached me.

"Are you okay?" I asked.

He was out of breath. "I'm fine," Fernando finally said.

"Oh good!" I said.

"I'm so lucky you're my friend," he said.

Is there a moral to my story about Fernando? I don't know. All I know is that he is a wonderful friend even though we are very different. And wouldn't the world be a boring place if we were all exactly the same? I think so. What do you think?

The man had read the book perhaps a hundred times since his reanimation. He'd found the battered cardboard box with his meager, government-issued belongings in the transitional housing he lived in before starting his first job and had enough money to rent an apartment. And each time he read the book, he heard the soft voice of an older woman with an accent similar to Faustina's mother's. But the man did not recognize the voice in his head—he had no idea to whom it belonged.

The man turned to the frontispiece of the book. Below the title was the name FERNANDO OCHOA written in block letters in alternating green and red crayon. He traced each letter with his right index finger. The man closed the book, examined the cover one more time—appreciating the colorful painting of the smiling young ferret with his friend, the beetle—then carefully placed it back into the battered cardboard box, closed the lid, and set it on the desk rather than returning it to the drawer. He then touched the business card as if to make certain it was still there. The man pulled out his phone and looked at Faustina's flight schedule for tomorrow. He knew that he should explain his plan to her in person, not by text or phone. But Faustina needed to prepare for her deposition, so it would need to wait until tomorrow night when she was back in town. The man turned off the desk lamp with a loud click.

Chapter Fifteen

THE MAN CLOSED HIS apartment door and entered the cool evening. He stretched his legs and twirled his arms in three clockwise circles. The man took a deep breath, put on his hoodie, and then started on his nightly run. He turned left on Hurlbut Street toward Pasadena Avenue and then turned left again. The man let his legs stretch out in long strides as his muscles slowly warmed up. He concentrated on his breathing. The man imagined Faustina's beautiful face and wondered how she would react when he made his request of her. Would she storm out of the room? Would she smile and say, *Yes, of course, how could you even doubt my decision*? Or would Faustina remain silent and simply stare at this man who would dare to ask her for such a thing?

NBC NIGHTLY NEWS SATURDAY WITH JOSÉ DÍAZ-BALART

JOSÉ DÍAZ-BALART: In other news, early this morning, the FBI raided the headquarters of one of the nation's largest reanimation facilities in Oxnard, California, seizing computer hard drives and records a month after President Cadwallader formally shut down the industry, though allowing for a repurposing of the technology. For more, we turn to NBC correspondent Emilie Ikeda for the story from Oxnard. Hello, Emilie.

EMILIE IKEDA: Hello, José.

JOSÉ DÍAZ-BALART: What can you tell us about this FBI raid?

EMILIE IKEDA: Well, José, the scene here at Clerval Industries in Oxnard is now calm, but as you can see in this tape from earlier this morning, the FBI was swift and thorough. I have with me president and CEO of Clerval, Akilah Hosseini, who agreed to answer a few questions for us. Ms. Hosseini, why would the FBI raid your facilities, and do you think it was politically motivated?

AKILAH HOSSEINI: Thank you, Emilie. We at Clerval Industries have always followed protocol when reanimation was legal, and we have complied with the new law and stopped our reanimation program with a move toward using the technological breakthroughs for other medical treatments, such as multiple transplant surgical techniques.

EMILIE IKEDA: But what have been the allegations, if you know, to support the FBI search?

AKILAH HOSSEINI: Well, there were some breaches in protocol early on in the reanimation program, that's true across the industry, but we at Clerval Industries moved quickly to put in place best practices and prevent any further breaches, and to cure past breaches where possible.

EMILIE IKEDA: What sort of breaches?

AKILAH HOSSEINI: Well, you know, the most common breach involved a few rogue employees making contact with reanimation subjects after reanimation and sharing personal information about the subjects' past lives, that sort of thing. All done with good intentions but against protocol. But again, we moved quickly and put in a fail-safe system to prevent this from happening again in the future. There have been no recent reports of these kinds of breaches.

EMILIE IKEDA: Then why has the FBI gotten involved now?

AKILAH HOSSEINI: I hate to say it, but I do think it's political. With those midterms looming, I think the raid was meant to grab headlines and make a political point. But it's not fair to our employees, who worked hard under the prior law and are now readjusting under the current reanimation ban. And even with the repurposing of the technology after the ban, we did have to trim our workforce to be leaner and more efficient to adjust to the new situation. But over time, we may be able to ramp up again as new breakthroughs are made.

EMILIE IKEDA: Next steps for you?

AKILAH HOSSEINI: We will continue to fully cooperate with the FBI because, quite frankly, we have nothing to hide. And if we find any additional breaches, we will deal appropriately and swiftly with those then.

EMILIE IKEDA: Thank you, Ms. Hosseini. José, back to you.

JOSÉ DÍAZ-BALART: Thank you, Emilie. Interesting report. Let's see how all of this develops.

Chapter Sixteen

THE MAN ENTERED THE Walgreens and strode to the back of the store. He saw the line and was relieved that only a woman and her daughter were in the queue. He had seen them before at the pharmacy, so he nodded to them. They stopped chatting, looked at the man, and simultaneously offered him a smile. When the man took his place behind them, the daughter—who looked no older than eleven or twelve to the man—spoke in Spanish to her mother. The man listened intently, pleased by the gentle manner she had with her mother. The daughter reassured her mother that the pharmacist would have a solution to her mother's reaction to the medication. The mother said she needed the medication for her heart, and she was afraid that the pharmacist might tell her to stop taking it altogether. The pharmacist suddenly said, "Next customer!" The mother and daughter approached the pharmacist, and the daughter took control of the conversation.

"My mother is taking this medicine," said the daughter as she handed the pharmacist a small plastic bottle. "She takes it for her heart, but it's making her swell in her wrists and ankles. And it is uncomfortable."

The pharmacist smiled and examined the bottle. As the pharmacist started to offer an opinion, the man looked up at the fluorescent lights that buzzed softly but relentlessly. He counted the number of tiles that surrounded the rectangular light fixture. *One, two, three, four, five, six, seven, eight, nine, ten.* An even ten. Three on the long sides of the rectangle, two each on the short sides. The same as last time, of course. The man blinked and looked down again at the woman and her daughter as the pharmacist handed the bottle back to the daughter, smiled, and said, "Tell your mother not to worry; her doctor will likely change the dosage, so call her doctor when you get back home to get the ball rolling."

"Thank you," said the girl. Her mother smiled and nodded at the pharmacist, a look of relief spreading across her face. The mother and daughter turned and walked away.

"Next in line," said the pharmacist.

The man came up to the counter. He noticed for the first time that the normally empty countertop now sported a large, plastic grinning jack-o'-lantern filled with mini Tootsie Rolls. The man looked into the pharmacist's eyes, gave his name, and asked for the second half of his medication. The pharmacist nodded and went back to the bins of prepared prescriptions. The man counted the bins: six across, five from floor to ceiling. Thirty bins total. The same as his last visit. The pharmacist came back to the counter empty-handed, typed something into the computer, and then shook his head. The man's left hand trembled, and beads of perspiration emerged on his forehead and upper lip.

"I am so sorry," said the pharmacist. "There is still a shortage of that medication. As I said the last time you were here, there's been a run on it because of that law the president signed. You know, a hoarding, and some supply chain issues. We simply don't have it in stock."

"But you only filled half my prescription the last time I was here, and I need the other half," said the man. "You told me that it would 'blow over in a week or two, and the supply will loosen up again.' Those were your exact words. I'm running out."

The pharmacist looked down at the countertop. The man waited for an answer.

"I shouldn't say this," began the pharmacist, keeping his eyes trained on an ink stain, "but you might consider other alternatives just until the supply loosens up."

The man shifted between his left foot and his right. "Alternatives?"

"There's a fear—that is really unfounded, if you ask me—that the manufacturers will stop making the drug," said the pharmacist as he looked up to meet the man's eyes. "But I am certain that will pass in time. Just like the run on toilet paper, flour, bottled water, meat, and other things during the early part of the pandemic, remember?"

The man did not remember because the pandemic happened before his reanimation. But he nodded anyway, since he had read about the bizarre hoarding that had no relation to actual shortages.

"What alternatives do I have?" said the man.

"Until it sorts itself out," said the pharmacist in a gentle voice, "you could ration your medication—you know, cut your pills in half—just so you don't go cold turkey."

The man nodded. There was logic to this solution.

"And as I said last time, there will likely be a generic soon," said the pharmacist. "Anyway, the good thing is you don't have to pay until the rest of your supply is here."

"Yes," said the man. "Okay. I will consider the alternative. Thank you."

"You're very welcome," said the pharmacist. "There's one alternative I do not suggest, however."

"What's that?"

"Don't buy stuff off the internet. There's all kinds of unscrupulous sellers out there who are peddling dangerous fake pills. I saw a horrible story on the news the other night. Let's just say you don't want to take that risk."

The man nodded and looked at the pharmacist. The pharmacist smiled and said, "Next in line!" The man turned and stepped away from the counter. He averted his eyes from the other customers and quickened his stride. He felt his throat closing, and he gulped at the cool air as he left the pharmacy.

The man found his car and got in. He closed his eyes and rubbed his temples. The man thought about what the pharmacist had said, cutting his pills in half. That would have to do for now. The man opened his eyes and blinked. *Okay*, he told himself. *That's what I'll do.* He closed his eyes again and conjured up Faustina's beautiful face in his mind's eye. The man's breathing slowed. His grimace slowly morphed into a small smile. After three minutes, the man opened his eyes, started his car, slowly backed out of his spot, and eased himself toward the parking lot's exit.

Chapter Seventeen

ARTHUR PAGE BROWN DESIGNED the San Francisco Ferry Building in 1892. A transplanted New Yorker, the young architect didn't live long enough to see the completion of his grand design. Two years before the Ferry Building's opening in 1898, Brown died at his Burlingame home, succumbing to severe injuries suffered in a runaway horse-and-buggy accident. He was thirty-seven years old. Brown left behind his wife, Lucy, and three children. Lucy and her six siblings were the children of Sara Agnes Rice Pryor and Roger Atkinson Pryor of Petersburg, Virginia. Roger had been a general in the Confederate army but started a new life for his family after the Civil War by moving to New York City. Roger became a successful attorney and prospered, eventually becoming active in Democratic Party politics. His hard work and political connections culminated in his appointment as a justice to the New York State Supreme Court. Roger was among a number of influential Southerners who had relocated to the North and became known as the "Confederate carpetbaggers," though he eventually renounced the Confederacy. His wife, Sara Agnes, also added to the city's social and intellectual fabric by becoming active in civic affairs, founding several heritage organizations, and writing novels, histories, and memoirs. Her first memoir, *Reminiscences of Peace and War*, was enthusiastically embraced by the United Daughters of the Confederacy, which encouraged Southern women writers to defend the Southern cause. Sara Agnes promoted the idea that the Civil War had nothing to do with slavery, but that the average Southern soldier fought to resist the Northern invasion. She died in 1912 at the age of eighty-one, predeceasing her husband by seven years.

The Ferry Building had been the second-busiest transit terminal in the world—second only to London's Charing Cross—until the 1930s, when the Bay Bridge and Golden Gate Bridge were completed. The magnificent structure suffered decades of decline until it was reimagined as a world-class food market and home to Book Passage, one of Faustina's favorite bookstores in the Bay Area. As a law student at the University of San Francisco School of Law, she would escape legal studies and browse the bookstore's extensive collection of novels and short story collections. And a few steps from Book Passage was the restaurant Cholita Linda, where Faustina would inevitably order a delicious plate of picadillo and an icy agua fresca. Hours would slip by as she got lost in a new book and slowly consumed a meal and drink that reminded Faustina of home. She eventually would head back to her apartment and get down to the business of studying law, though refreshed and feeling more whole because of her visit to the Ferry Building, whose history Faustina did not know.

And today, thirteen years after graduating from law school, after the deposition that ended early and on a pleasanter note than she had expected—with opposing counsel suggesting they discuss settlement very, very soon—Faustina had ordered her favorite dish of picadillo but with a Modelo Negra rather than an agua fresca, since she had earned a nice beer with her meal. Because she was famished, Faustina had reversed her traditional practice of first visiting the bookstore. But once refreshed, she promised herself a visit to Book Passage to look for that perfect literary purchase to keep her entertained in the Lyft, at the airport, and then on the flight back home. For now, Faustina enjoyed the food, drink, and bustle of the lunchtime crowd.

And just as it did in law school, this simple dish of sautéed ground beef with green peppers, tomatoes, and onions served with a side of rice and pinto beans brought Faustina back to her childhood in Los Angeles, where her mother brilliantly stretched a limited budget to feed her three daughters—Carolina, Belén, and the youngest, Faustina. The tight budget was not for want of employment. Verónica taught first grade at Saint Thomas the Apostle Grammar School where the three girls were enrolled, thus allowing for discounted tuition. And her father, Agustín, had a solid unionized job as a mechanic for the Metro as a team leader, doing his part keeping Los Angeles's massive bus system healthy and running. But life was expensive. The mortgage on their small house plus clothes, food, insurance, car payments, and everything else kept them on a tight budget. Her mother's picadillo and similar budget-smart meals like chilaquiles helped stretch the household's dollars. And this frugality served the family well when the three Godínez daughters attended college and—in

Faustina's case—law school. So, in a sense, Faustina's success rested on the simple but delicious Mexican dishes of picadillo, chilaquiles, and other frugal meals.

"Fausti!"

Faustina's reverie was shattered by this somewhat strained male voice that rose above the din of the lunchtime crowd. Only one person called her Fausti. She looked up from her picadillo and beer. Nicolás struggled to get past the hungry patrons but finally broke through and found a spot to plant his feet near Faustina's table. Faustina did not stand to greet her ex-husband. She simply looked up from her lunch, nodded, and waited.

"What a surprise to see you up in the city!" said Nicolás, maintaining his delight despite meeting Faustina's deadpan acknowledgment.

"Hi, Nick," said Faustina. She knew her ex-husband hated being called Nick in the same way she hated being called Fausti.

"May I sit?" said Nicolás as he plopped down on the chair directly across from Faustina.

"Make yourself at home."

"That looks good! Maybe I should order a plate."

"I'm almost done," said Faustina as she lifted her fork and took a mouthful of rice mixed with beans. "The line is long, so by the time your order is ready, I will be long gone."

"Right. I'll get lunch later. How often do I run into my beautiful ex-wife?"

Faustina unsuccessfully suppressed a cringe. They sat in silence as she continued to eat. Finally Faustina said, "How is Delia?"

"Oh, really great," said Nicolás, "I guess."

"You guess? You don't know how your wife is?"

"Ex-wife," he said. "Been almost six months since the divorce became final."

"So you now have two ex-wives?" said Faustina, this time attempting to suppress a smirk, again unsuccessfully.

"But it's all good, all good," said Nicolás, somewhat convincingly. "I took your advice."

"On what?"

"You know, I got some direction in my career, finally, after bouncing around from job to job."

"Nick, we divorced ten years ago."

"Yes, but…"

"It took you a decade and another ex-wife to finally listen to me?"

"Okay, okay, I know I sound like a loser, but I really did it!"

"Did what?"

"I enrolled in a paralegal program at Cal State East Bay."

Faustina chuckled. "Well, good for you, Nick."

"I know it's not law school, like what you did…"

"It's not, but it's a real profession, not like some of your other schemes. Some of which were a bit sketchy, if you want me to be honest about it."

Nicolás nodded. "You were always honest."

"Did any of it rub off?"

"Ouch," said Nicolás. "The past is the past. I've matured."

"Is that why you have two ex-wives now?"

"I repeat: ouch!"

Faustina took a long drink from her beer. "Okay, okay. Felicidades on your new start. I hope it goes well and that you like being a paralegal."

"You mean that?"

"I never lie," said Faustina. "You know that."

"Yep," said Nicolás. "If there's one thing I know about you, it's that you are truthful to a fault."

"Try it sometime. You might like it."

FAUSTINA'S PLANE LANDED AT LAX that night at 7:46 p.m. The relatively short flight felt even shorter because she had visited Book Passage after Nicolás had left her to finish her lunch, and she purchased one of Yxta Maya Murray's short story collections from a few years back, *The World Doesn't Work That Way, but It Could*. She had gotten lost in the short stories' biting humor, satirical social commentary, and gorgeous sentences, so the one-hour flight was over before she knew it. Faustina marveled at how a full-time law professor such as Murray could have so many books to her name—novels, short fiction, nonfiction. And she was a playwright too! How did Murray balance two disparate careers so well? Why couldn't she do that? But then Faustina remembered a quote from Oscar Wilde: "Be yourself; everyone else is already taken." No use comparing herself to Murray.

As Faustina drove home, she went over her conversation with Nicolás. Two ex-wives in ten years! She wondered if she should have warned Delia about Nicolás's wandering eye and expert ability to charm his way out of any situation. But Delia was a grown-ass woman, and besides, Faustina suspected that Delia and Nicolás had screwed around before Faustina finally got wise and filed the dissolution papers. So Delia very likely had firsthand knowledge of her then-new man's cheatin' ways. What's sauce for the goose and all that.

Faustina drove up the driveway. She jumped when her

headlights hit a figure that stood in front of her garage door. Then she recognized him. The man hugged a battered cardboard box to his chest. He moved to one side as the garage door opened and Faustina parked. She opened her door and got out.

"You scared the shit out of me," said Faustina as she closed the car door and searched for her house keys in her large black purse. "You shouldn't do that to people. Maybe I had a gun and would have shot you."

"You don't have a gun."

"I know, I know. But you get my point."

"Sorry," said the man. "I wanted to tell you something."

"It couldn't wait until tomorrow?"

"No," said the man. "It's too important."

"Okay," said Faustina as she opened the door to the house. "Come on in, but I want to get out of this suit first and into something more comfortable. We can have a drink and talk. I'm all about listening to men today."

Chapter Eighteen

THE MAN SAT IN a wingback chair, the shadows almost making him disappear as a single standing lamp offered the only source of light in Faustina's living room. She had poured two glasses of Riesling, set the wineglasses and wine bottle on the coffee table's glass top, and went to the bedroom to change out of her suit and into something more comfortable. The man set the cardboard box down on the coffee table, reached for his wineglass, and took a long drink. Within a few seconds, he finished his wine but clung to the wineglass. He sighed, reached for the bottle, and poured a generous second serving for himself.

"Liquid courage," said Faustina as she entered the living room wearing sweatpants and a Chicano Batman T-shirt emblazoned with a large red rose that she'd purchased when they performed in Phoenix last year. She plopped down on the sofa on the other side of the coffee table across from the man. It had been a long day, and she wanted a little space.

"What's in the box?"

The man took another long drink and nodded toward the box. "Please, look."

Faustina took a drink of her wine, then reached for the box. She opened it slowly, peered inside, then looked up at the man.

"A kid's book?"

"Yes."

Faustina took another drink, then reached into the box and pulled out the book. She examined each page and quickly became absorbed by the simple story. Faustina didn't know what she felt. When she finished reading it to herself, Faustina closed the book and carefully placed it back in the box.

"Who is Fernando Ochoa?"

The man shifted in his seat.

Faustina leaned forward. "Is that you, before the, er, your…"

"Reanimation," the man whispered.

Faustina coughed, took another drink, and refilled her wineglass before answering, "Yes, that's what I meant. Before your reanimation."

"I think so."

"Where did you get it?"

The man haltingly explained how he had found the battered cardboard box with his paltry first belongings in the transitional housing where he'd lived for a short while after being reanimated. But he did not tell Faustina that each time he read the book, he heard in his mind the soft voice of an older woman with an accent similar to Faustina's mother's. That voice haunted him.

"Who do you think gave it to you?"

The man hesitated, then slowly retrieved the business card from his shirt pocket and handed it to Faustina.

"'Dr. Marco Prietto,'" read Faustina. "'Clerval Industries.' That's one of the big reanimation centers in California."

"Yes, it's in Oxnard."

"'When you are ready,'" read Faustina. "Ready for what?"

"I think it means when I am ready to learn more. About me."

Faustina handed the business card to the man, who studied it again before putting it back into his shirt pocket.

"And are you?" said Faustina.

The man took a drink, put his wineglass down, and sat back in his chair. He let out a soft sigh, trained his eyes on the cardboard box, and said in a gentle but determined voice, "Ever since my reanimation, I have lived in a fog. I know how to do things. I read books. I work in a law firm. I pay my bills and taxes and go to the grocery store, and I can prepare meals—not fancy ones but meals nonetheless—and drive a car, and clean my apartment, and shave, and take my medications, and do everything that most people can do. I am not a stupid man. And I have feelings. Sort of. Feelings that don't quite feel complete. They are shadows of feelings. Memories of feelings. But they are feelings; I know that for certain. But I don't know where any of that—any of me—came from. I have no sense of what it means to be me. I feel like I'm half a man. Am I making sense?"

The man turned his eyes from the cardboard box to Faustina before continuing: "Do you understand how it feels to be without any sense of why you are the way you are? To have no memory or understanding of where you came from? I have no family. But I know I had a family—I think. That kid's book tells me that someone cared for me, maybe even loved me. Was that someone a mother? A father? Maybe a sister or a brother? Do you have any idea what that does to a person? I know what it's done to me. It's left me hollow. I guess I'll never really know if I was already like that, before the reanimation. Maybe I was always a hollow man. But I don't think so. But I do think it has made me shut down in some way and not fully participate in life. I've been going through the motions. Until I met you, Faustina. You have given me a need or desire or maybe I don't know what, but somehow something has been revived or rekindled in me to find out... to find out... to find out... where I come from. Because if I can do that... if I can do that... if I can do that—maybe I will find out who I am or who I was. Does that make sense, Faustina? I don't know what I feel about you because I am broken. But I know I feel good being with you. I know I have enjoyed knowing your family. I like your friends. But I need something of my own, like what you have, Faustina. I am lost. I don't know what else to do but to call the doctor and see what he has to say. But I might not like what I hear. I am scared. That feeling is real and full and complete. I am scared. I am scared. The doctor might tell me things that are horrible. But I need to find out, even if I end up regretting what I learn. Does that make any sense, Faustina? Please tell me if that makes sense?"

They sat in silence for a long while. The man could hear the old mahogany Berlin clock on the mantel tick softly. Finally Faustina nodded.

"I think so," she began. "I think so. And I like being with you, so there's that, right? That's not a such bad thing when two people like being with each other. That's something that people—reanimated or not—can cherish and appreciate. Right? So I know you want more than that, something that tells you more about you. I get that... yes... okay, I can say that I get that. But..."

"But what?"

"What do you want from me?"

The man nodded. "If I go see this doctor, would you be willing to come with me?"

Faustina stood, grabbed her wineglass, and moved away from the man to the far end of the living room, into the shadows. She took a long drink and folded her arms across her chest.

"That's a hell of a thing to ask," Faustina began in a soft voice, without anger or vindictiveness. "And I'm not saying that to be mean. I'm just saying what I feel, nothing more."

"I wish I could say that I understand," said the man. "But I don't know what the normal thing is. I don't know if the me before reanimation would ask you to do this."

"Ah, but there's the rub, right? If you were you before reanimation, you wouldn't have a cardboard box with a kid's book and a business card for a doctor who might be able to fill you in on your history, who you were, where you came from."

The man nodded.

"So let's not bother saying what if," said Faustina. "In the here and now, it's one hell of a thing to ask of anyone. To ask of me. Look, I like you, yes, but we've known each other for weeks, not years, and we're not living together; we're certainly not married. But we click for some reason. I do like you, I do. So I don't blame you for asking. I suppose that if I were in your position, I'd do the same," she said before taking another long drink of wine. "So don't get me wrong, okay? I'm just trying to wrap my head around it. This is as new to me as it is to you. Get that?"

"I understand," said the man. He drained the last bit of wine, then stood. "I can go now."

Faustina walked out of the shadows and stood by the lamp. "No, it might be better if you stay. You've been drinking, and there's still a bit more wine in the bottle, so we shouldn't let that go to waste, right?" She smiled.

"You make a compelling argument," said the man with a smile.

"Because I'm a kick-ass lawyer," said Faustina as she reached for the bottle and poured the last of the wine into their glasses. "And I admit that I am annoyed, really annoyed, maybe a little pissed with you. But what the hell? Maybe this is our first real argument."

"Is that a good thing?"

"Well, it's a thing."

They stood in silence. Faustina then laughed a little and held up her wineglass in a toast. "Here's to asking too damn much of your new lady friend."

The man held up his wineglass and clinked it with Faustina's.

"So what's next?" said the man.

"We drink and maybe have some makeup sex since, you know, we did just kind of argue, right? And we should talk more, of course. Because right now I'm too tired to give you an answer."

"Deal," said the man. "And thank you."

"Por nada," said Faustina. "No promises. But I am willing to discuss. You've kind of grown on me, even if you really pissed me off just now."

The man chuckled. "That is the nicest thing anyone has ever said to me."

"Oh, muchacho," said Faustina as she came closer to the man, "you need to get around more."

Chapter Nineteen

THE MAN DID NOT go for a run that evening. He slept in Faustina's bed, curled up behind her after making love. Their soft snores filled the bedroom. But as the night wore on, the man's legs jerked, and he emitted a noise that sounded like he wanted to scream.

TRANSCRIPT OF OVAL OFFICE MEETING, OCT. 29, 9:45 A.M.

POTUS BRIEFED BY COMMUNICATIONS TEAM: B. ESKANDARI, M. VAN GELDEREN, T. LUNDGREN, J. TOMA

POTUS:	Where are we?
ESKANDARI:	In the generic, Trafalgar has us ahead six points as of this morning. And Rasmussen has us up five.
POTUS:	Good. No surprises there. But what about the real pollsters? What does ABC/Washington Post say? Quinnipiac?
ESKANDARI:	Nothing new from Quinnipiac yet, but three days ago they had us up three with an upward trendline, and ABC/Washington Post also had us up by three yesterday.
VAN GELDEREN:	Yes, upward trendline on most polls.
ESKANDARI:	Yep, upward trendline overall.
LUNDGREN:	[UNINTELLIGIBLE]
POTUS:	So the ads are working, right? And keeping Shithead relegated to talking about infrastructure was a smart move, I don't mind saying.
LUNDGREN:	Smart decision.
POTUS:	Damn straight.
ESKANDARI:	And signing that bill—the reanimation ban—is polling really well still.

TOMA:	Though Nate Silver still calls the midterms a toss-up, especially the Senate races.
ESKANDARI:	Right, but he always hedges his bets. He doesn't want egg on his face.
POTUS:	Motherfucking asshole. I hate that guy. So smug. Always gives himself wiggle room. He should stick to poker.
ESKANDARI:	But Silver still says the midterms are for us to lose, so there's that narrative.
POTUS:	My goddamn Scottish terrier could have said that.
VAN GELDEREN:	But Lucky died last year.
POTUS:	I know fucking Lucky died last year. And he still could have said that.
ESKANDARI:	I miss Lucky.
POTUS:	Lucky was smarter than Nate Silver, and more likeable too. Okay, what else can we do to goose our midterm numbers? Anyone?
TOMA:	I think we've maxed out on the reanimation ban, but there is something that, er, maybe the DOJ can do. But we need to keep the White House fingerprints off of it.
POTUS:	I like what I'm hearing. Go on.
TOMA:	Well, maybe a few high-profile prosecutions or investigations could help us . . .
VAN GELDEREN:	You, know, go after some of these reanimation centers for violating the ban, or for violating their prior reanimation licenses. You know, breaches of the stitcher protocols.

TOMA:	Like that one center that was raided by the FBI.
ESKANDARI:	Clerval.
TOMA:	Right, Clerval. They've got to find something in the hard drives, right? Emails, whatever. Some kind of protocol breach.
POTUS:	But the AG hasn't said anything, right?
LUNDGREN:	Right. She's kind of cautious on announcing.
POTUS:	I fucking know that. Biggest goddamn mistake appointing McCluskie. A regular Girl Scout. She doesn't know she works for me. Stupid bitch.
ESKANDARI:	Well, technically, the AG doesn't work for the president . . .
POTUS:	Spare me . . .
ESKANDARI:	But there might be pressure to act, and to announce a prosecution or investigation, based on what I see on Fox. There's a drumbeat starting.
LUNDGREN:	Yes, a drumbeat.
POTUS:	[UNINTELLIGIBLE]
VAN GELDEREN:	We could set up an informal, off-the-radar meeting with McCluskie.
POTUS:	We should do that soon.
ESKANDARI:	You have dinner open on Thursday. Maybe something low-key, here in the White House, just you two.
POTUS:	Yep. Nice and private.
TOMA:	But we can't set that up through White House scheduling. Can't leave a trail.

ESKANDARI: Should be a call from you.

POTUS: Yep.

VAN GELDEREN: Maybe hint at something big in her future.

LUNDGREN: Yes.

POTUS: Like what?

ESKANDARI: Next Supreme Court vacancy.

LUNDGREN: If she plays ball.

POTUS: Right . . .

LUNDGREN: Justice Williams is barely hanging on . . .

POTUS: The fucking walking dead . . .

VAN GELDEREN: Could have a vacancy as soon as next year.

ESKANDARI: Williams is almost ninety and had those strokes.

POTUS: Why do they hang on like that? No fucking dignity. Maybe he's a stitcher! Ha! That's pretty funny. I make myself laugh.

TOMA: Not certain why he hangs on. I'd retire and enjoy the rest of my life.

POTUS: I'll tell you why. It's a fucking easy gig, that's why. The law clerks do all the work. The fucking easiest job in the world with all that prestige, and the paycheck and speaking fees. Lucky could do that job.

TOMA: But Lucky is dead.

POTUS: And so is fucking Williams!

TOMA: Not quite, but yeah . . .

POTUS: Damn right, yeah.

TOMA: Back to McCluskie.

POTUS: Yes. Let me call her today.

TOMA: [UNINTELLIGIBLE]

POTUS: Yep.

LUNDGREN: And if we get the AG to announce some high-profile prosecutions or an investigation, or even a grand jury indictment soon, we can cut some spots and let the National Committee run them under its name.

ESKANDARI: We can cut those now and just drop in video of the AG later, when her press conference happens.

LUNDGREN: We could just use video from other AG announcements and do a voiceover so we can move faster.

POTUS: I fucking like that. Fast.

TOMA: We can do that.

POTUS: Okay, I have to meet with the goddamn British prime minister in an hour, so go forth and fucking make this shit happen.

LUNDGREN: Yes, we can do that.

POTUS: Well?

ESKANDARI: Well what?

POTUS: Go fucking make it happen! I'll call the AG now.

—END OF TRANSCRIPT—

Chapter Twenty

THEY SAT IN SILENCE at Faustina's breakfast table. The man appreciated the brightness of this small and cozy room that opened up to the kitchen. The space felt safe, nourishing, tranquil. Faustina had decorated the walls with three framed colorful prints by three different artists. One in particular enthralled the man: hundreds of people of all ages and sizes stared back at the man against a cityscape that looked like the skyscrapers of downtown Los Angeles. Some figures played instruments; many kept their eyes shut tight in sublime peace, perhaps entranced by the music they or others played. One small figure was dressed as a skeleton. At the bottom in pencil was the artwork's title, *The Eternal Getdown*, with the artist's large, loopy signature of *José Ramírez* set off in the right-hand corner. At the left-hand corner the artist had written in the same pencil *22/25*. The man thought about this number. This meant that in twenty-four other kitchens or bedrooms or living rooms, this very same print might be adorning other people's walls.

The man counted to twenty-four and smiled. This colorful print connected him to others he has never met, at least to his knowledge. He then focused on the lone skeletal figure, who seemed to smile back at him.

The man sipped his coffee. He turned to watch Faustina prepare breakfast at the oven. He had offered to help, but she said no, sit, have coffee, and save your energy for a discussion. So the man complied. Faustina seemed less irritated with him. But an uneasiness lurked beneath this domestic scene. The man's sleep had been fitful last night, with his recurring dream intruding yet again. The man thought that making love with Faustina and holding her tightly throughout the night might help, but the dream came to him unhindered. In fact, if anything, it was more vivid, more terrifying, more confounding than the other times he had experienced it. He blamed the wine and something else that he could not name. He looked down at his coffee and tried to clear his mind.

"Okay, guapo," said Faustina, interrupting the man's thoughts, "the breakfast of champions is served."

The man looked up from his coffee. "It smells good."

"It should," said Faustina turning toward the man. "Nothing beats huevos con weenies for Mexican comfort food."

"I don't know if I've had that before."

"You said that at the brunch with my family," said Faustina as she scooped their breakfast out of the steaming skillet and onto two plates. "How could that be? What kind of Chicano are you?"

"I didn't say I never had it," said the man as Faustina placed a plate in front of him. "It looks familiar, but I don't know if I ever ate this."

Faustina prepared the corn tortillas on the oven's burners

and looked as if she regretted her accusation. She wrapped the hot tortillas in a white towel, placed it on the table, sat, and poured herself a cup of coffee.

"Lo siento," said Faustina. "That was rude of me. Here, try some salsa on it. I got it from Trader Joe's and it's actually pretty good. White people be stealing our Mexican secrets!"

The man scooped three spoonsful of salsa onto his eggs, then grabbed a tortilla from the towel, tore a piece off the tortilla, and used it with his fork to scoop a mouthful of eggs onto the tortilla.

"Now that's how a Chicano eats." Faustina laughed. "Forgive me for doubting you."

"That's good," said the man through a mouthful of food. "Really, really good."

The man closed his eyes and enjoyed the flavors and textures rolling around in his mouth. And then it happened: the man saw flashes of a face—an older woman—smiling at him. A shock ran through his body, and his eyes popped open.

"What's wrong?"

The man blinked, then swallowed what was left in his mouth. He stared blankly at Faustina.

"Are you okay?" said Faustina.

"I saw something," said the man as he kept his eyes trained on Faustina.

"Something?"

"A face."

"Whose face?"

"I don't know."

"You didn't recognize it?"

"No."

"Has this happened before?"

The man took a drink of coffee. "Yes, a few times."

"When was the last time?"

"When we had brunch. When we cooked chilaquiles, and I took my first taste of it."

Faustina touched the man's shoulder. "Let's finish breakfast, then go for a walk, okay?"

The man didn't answer.

"Do you want something else to eat?" said Faustina.

The man shook his head, then slowly started to eat again. Faustina took in a big breath, blinked, and then took a drink of coffee.

"I'm okay," said the man. "I'm okay."

THE MAN AND FAUSTINA entered Arlington Garden. A few families wandered about, bundled up against the still-chilly morning air. The botanical garden seemed to sway and sing in unison as the cool breeze picked up.

"I run near here all the time, but I've never noticed it," said the man. "At least, I don't think I noticed it. I guess I must have noticed something."

"I love this place," said Faustina as they crunched along the gravel pathway. "It's only about three acres, but it feels like it goes on forever, especially along the perimeter, where you can almost get lost in the trees and plants."

"I'd like to get lost for a while."

"Me too," said Faustina as she looped her left arm into the man's right. "You know, there used to be a mansion on this spot that was built over a hundred years ago by a guy named John Durand. Of course, it was known as the Durand Mansion."

"How did you know that?"

Faustina laughed. "One of my great adventures was volunteering as a docent here a couple of years ago. On weekends. I loved it because I got to enjoy these beautiful surroundings while being in charge of a group of tourists who were not armed with knowledge, at least not as much knowledge as I had."

"Knowledge is your superpower."

"Ha! That's pretty good. You surprise me sometimes."

"I do?"

Faustina guided the man toward a bench in a small clearing. They stopped in front of the bench and simultaneously leaned in to read the brass plaque on the top of the bench that read:

In loving memory of my husband, the poet
Robert Angel, 1951–2020
Who found inspiration in these gardens.
Mary Angel

"I keep forgetting to look up Robert Angel," said Faustina as she let go of the man's arm and slowly eased onto the bench. "I might ask at Vroman's next time I'm there looking for something new to read."

The man thought for a moment, then sat near Faustina.

"Do you think Robert Angel wrote a book of poetry?" said the man.

"Maybe. Don't know."

"Do you read a lot of poetry?"

"Some. Not as much as fiction, though," said Faustina as she looked up into the surrounding trees. "But when I do read poetry, I am often surprised at how much I like it. I recently read a collection by this Nicaraguan poet, what was his name?

Oh, yes, Salvatierra. That's it, León Salvatierra. I read an interview of him in the *Los Angeles Times* a few years ago and he
sounded so smart and thoughtful. He fled Nicaragua at age
fifteen to escape becoming a child soldier for the Sandinistas.
I can't imagine what he saw at such a young age. Anyway, I
eventually picked up his book—it's called *To the North*—but I
didn't read it for a few months. It just sat on my nightstand.
You know how it is. The TBR pile just grows and grows. But
then one night I opened it and started reading. Each poem was
in English with its Spanish translation following. Sometimes
I'd begin with the English before reading it in my not-so-good
Spanish. And sometimes I'd begin with the Spanish then move
to the English."

"Why?"

"I guess I liked feeling the difference between the languages.
Even the title of the book in Spanish has a different feel than the
English: *Al norte*. It's more musical; fewer words but the same
number of syllables. It sets a different tone, I guess."

"Tell me about the mansion that used to be here."

"Yes!" said Faustina. "But first, you should know that this
garden is the ancestral land of the Tongva peoples, renamed by
the Spanish as the Gabrieleño."

"Why?"

"Because colonizers just love renaming everything they
colonize. Junípero Serra founded the San Gabriel Mission, so
the Tongva got a new name to match the mission where they
were baptized against their will and forced to work the land.
You know, the usual colonizer shit. And of course, most of the
Tongva had no immunity for the colonizers' diseases, so a lot of
their population just died out."

"Oh."

"But I digress. The mansion you wanted to know about."

"Yes."

"Okay, you asked for it," said Faustina as she stood, then situated herself in front of the man. She cleared her throat, then began, "About a century after the mission system officially ended in California, this location became the home of a fifty-room mansion called the Durand House after the man who built it in the early twentieth century. John Durand was a wealthy wholesaler originally from the great city of Chicago. Durand wanted to replicate a baronial French château in his design. The original structure featured a red sandstone exterior, elaborate wood carvings, and lush gardens that included orange trees and tropical palms, which enjoyed Pasadena's temperate weather. The Durand House's extravagance prompted the *Los Angeles Times* to proclaim it as 'the most peculiar and at the same time the most lavishly finished residence not only in Southern California but in the whole country.' The mansion was unusual not only for its utter extravagance but also for such eccentric features as the master switch placed next to Mrs. Durand's bed that, when flipped, turned on 'every light in the house from cellar to roof,' apparently as a deterrence for would-be burglars."

"So strange."

"Yes, strange indeed, you handsome member of the audience," said Faustina. Then, in a stage whisper, she added: "Meet me when we're done and I'll give you a private tour, if you get my drift." She punctuated her offer with an exaggerated wink.

The man laughed. Faustina resumed her docent stance and voice.

"In any event," she continued, "this strangeness came to an end when Caltrans—that state agency that everyone loves to hate—purchased and demolished the Durand House in 1964. And of course, Caltrans being Caltrans, the state agency used the vacant lot to store heavy equipment during the construction of the Long Beach Freeway expansion. Otherwise the lot remained undeveloped and unused. But someone came up with the idea to lease the lot to Pasadena for city purposes. And what could be better for a city—other than affordable housing—than a beautiful park? Now the Arlington Garden is maintained by a group of nonprofit organizations as well as the city itself."

Faustina punctuated her speech with an exaggerated curtsy then returned to bench and sat near the man.

"¡Brava!" said the man as he clapped slowly.

"Thank you, thank you, my adoring public."

The man stopped clapping and fell into silence.

"But what about the garden itself?" he finally said.

"Ah, yes, points of interest. For that, we must stroll around so I may offer you a proper tour."

They stood. Faustina looped her left arm around the man's right, and she directed them away from the bench.

"As you can see," said Faustina as she dramatically gestured with her right hand, "Arlington Garden includes thousands and thousands of California-native plants such as sunflowers, poppies, cacti, and succulents; orchards of olive and orange trees; and many other examples of flora. And thanks to generous private donations and funding from the City of Pasadena itself, the garden also includes a wide variety of benches and tables for relaxing and communing with nature. And throughout, you will notice various stone birdbaths, statuary, and a craftsman-inspired tile fountain."

They approached a small forest of myrtle trees. Hundreds of multicolored paper notes fluttered from the branches. The man approached a myrtle and cupped one of the notes so that he could read it.

"'For Grammy's good health,'" read the man. "'I love my grammy.'" He released the note and watched it flutter again, like the hundreds of other notes on the myrtles.

"They usually ask for good health," said Faustina as she reached for another. "Or like this one: 'I wish for someone to love me for who I am.'"

"What are these trees?" said the man.

"Good question from the audience!" said Faustina as she positioned herself in front of the man to offer another docent explanation. "The crape myrtle trees that line this walk were originally part of Yoko Ono's interactive performance art project dubbed *Wish Tree*. All visitors to Arlington Garden are invited to participate by adding their own wishes to the trees."

Faustina curtsied, then looped her left arm around the man's right. They stood lost in their own thoughts as they watched the multitude of wishes flutter in the breeze.

"Have you ever put a wish on one of these trees?" asked the man.

"Do I look like someone who believes in magical wishes?" laughed Faustina.

"No."

"Well, truth be told, yes I have."

"Oh?"

"When my best friend from college, Angelica, got breast cancer. I put a note up for her asking for the chemo to work and make her better."

"Did she get better?"

"No," said Faustina as she closed her eyes. "There's no fucking magic in the world."

The man watched in silence as the breeze picked up, making

the notes flutter wildly. The breeze eventually subsided and the notes calmed to a gentle flutter.

"I'm sorry I asked you to come with me to see Dr. Marco Prietto," said the man.

"Forget about it," said Faustina as she opened her eyes and looked at the man. She unlinked her arm from his and stepped back a little. "I would have done the same. But the question is: Do you really want to see him? Are you ready to learn who you are—I mean, who you were?"

The man thought for a moment. The breeze grew stronger and the wishing notes fluttered petulantly.

"Yes," said the man. "I want to know."

"And why do you want me with you when you meet the doctor?"

The man sighed.

"Do you know?" said Faustina.

"Yes, I know."

"Well?"

"Because," said the man, "I am frightened about what I might learn."

Faustina looked intently at the man. "Anything else?" she said.

"And I trust you."

Faustina took in a deep breath. She moved closer to the man and looped her left arm into the man's right.

"Okay then," said Faustina. "Call the good doctor and let him know that you and I want to meet him."

The man stared at Faustina in disbelief.

"Well?" said Faustina.

"Thank you," said the man. "Thank you."

"I'm a full-service docent," said Faustina. "Guided tours and moral support and pretty good sex, if I might be so blunt."

The man laughed.

"And I'm pretty funny too."

"Yes," said the man. "You are."

Chapter Twenty-One

"I THINK THIS IS the place," said Faustina as she pulled in front of the well-kept house that was illuminated by a bright moon. "I wish the good doctor had agreed to meet at his office."

"He told me that since the FBI raid, Clerval Industries is being watched closely," said the man as he lifted the cardboard box from the floor to his lap. "Outside visitors especially so."

"Makes sense, but this feels creepy. Daytime in an office feels safer than nighttime at a private residence anytime in my book."

"But he's a doctor."

"Okay, okay," said Faustina as she turned off the car and unbuckled her seat belt. "Let's see what the good doctor has to say. I also have to pee really badly. A two-hour drive to Oxnard will do that to a girl. Traffic through the San Fernando Valley really sucked."

"I'm sure he will let you use his bathroom," said the man as he opened his car door.

"If he doesn't, this meeting ain't happening," said Faustina.

As they walked toward the house, they noticed the curtains move in the bay window.

"We're being watched," said Faustina.

"Maybe I scare him," said the man as he hugged the cardboard box tightly to his chest.

"Why?"

"My people have been getting a lot of bad press lately."

"Your people?"

The man looked at Faustina and smiled just a bit.

"Your sense of humor is improving by the hour," said Faustina.

They walked up the four steps to the small porch and stared at the front door. A large, grinning jack-o'-lantern sat on the left end of the porch.

"Someone likes Halloween," said Faustina.

"Well," said the man, "I guess someone should ring the doorbell or knock."

"Sounds like a logical choice. I vote for knocking. It's much more assertive. We need to approach from a position of strength."

"You're sounding like a lawyer."

"Guilty as charged."

The man raised his right hand, made a fist, and prepared to knock. But before he could, the door opened. In front of Faustina and the man stood a short, gray-haired man who held a black-and-white cat in his arms. He was boxy and neat like his house.

"Dr. Prietto, I presume," said Faustina.

Dr. Prietto looked at the man and then Faustina and then back at the man. He smiled and nodded. "Come in, please," he said as he stepped aside to let his guests in.

"Which way to your bathroom?" said Faustina as she entered.

"Oh, yes," said the doctor. "Down the hallway, on your left. We'll be over here in the living room."

Faustina nodded her thanks and walked quickly toward the bathroom. The doctor nodded back and then guided the man down a different hallway to the living room. They entered a capacious but cluttered area whose major furnishing seemed to be books of all sizes on wall-to-ceiling bookshelves and every horizontal surface including the floor. Side one of Tierra's *City Nights* filled the room at a low volume from a turntable hidden in the shadows. The doctor set his cat down on the couch and then removed about a dozen books from the same couch and carefully stacked them in a corner of the room near another stack of books. The doctor motioned to the man to sit near the cat. The man obliged. The cat looked up at the man, blinked, licked its lips, and closed its eyes to sleep. The man set the cardboard box down on the coffee table, which was already covered with various books. He turned to the curled-up feline and scratched the back of its head. The cat seemed to appreciate this gesture immensely.

"Quetzi likes you," said the doctor.

"Quetzi?" said the man.

"Short for Quetzalcoatl. The Plumed Serpent! You know, the greatest of the Aztec gods."

"Oh."

"May I get you a drink?"

"No, thank you."

The doctor walked to a small table that groaned under various bottles and glasses. "I could use another little splash," he said as he refilled his glass with an amber liquid from a cut-crystal decanter. "Doctor's orders!" he chuckled as he retrieved his now-full glass and settled into a large leather wingback chair across from the couch. He took a long drink and exhaled loudly. "¡Híjole!" the doctor exclaimed to himself as the booze warmed his throat.

"Oh, there you both are," said Faustina as she entered the living room. "I found the kitchen and another little room before I found you gentlemen. I guess I was distracted when you pointed to where you were going. A full bladder will do that to me."

The doctor stood and held up his glass. "Drink?"

"A little happy juice would be nice," said Faustina as she made her way to the small table. "A fine collection of adult beverages."

"There's ice in the bucket there," said the doctor as he sat again and smiled at this beautiful woman's unabashed desire to have a drink.

Faustina dropped three ice cubes into a glass and examined her options until she found the bottle she wanted. "Ooh, you have Johnnie Walker Blue Label!" she cooed as she snatched up the bottle and poured a healthy glass of whiskey. "I deserve a treat after all of that driving," she added as she returned to the couch and settled in next to the man.

"I'm glad you called me," said the doctor. "You're saving me from being a superfluous man."

The man clutched his knees and nodded. Faustina enjoyed her drink.

The doctor smiled at Faustina and took a drink as a sign of camaraderie. He then gingerly balanced his glass on a pile of books on the coffee table and reached for the cardboard box. The doctor placed the box on his lap and slowly opened it. He smiled.

"Why do I have this book?" said the man.

"I put it with your new belongings when you were reanimated, of course," said the doctor.

"But why?" said Faustina.

"What does it mean?" said the man.

"Two very different questions," said the doctor. "Which one
shall I answer first?"

Faustina turned to the man and waited for him to respond.

"Answer her question first," said the man after a few seconds of thought.

"I'm glad you chose that first, because the second question is
a bit harder to answer," said the doctor as he returned the book
to the cardboard box. He took a long drink and sat in silence for
almost a full minute. Finally he said, "The short answer is what
I alluded to before. I don't want to be a superfluous man."

"Wait," said Faustina. "You were the doctor who worked on
his reanimation, right?"

"I am, along with my team, yes."

"So how could you be a superfluous man if you gave
him life?"

"It is one thing to set something—or someone—in motion;
it is something else to give that act of creation meaning."

"I don't understand," said the man.

The doctor drained his glass, stood, and walked to his make-
shift bar. He refreshed his drink, returned to his chair, and took
another drink before considering how he could answer. The
doctor breathed in deeply as he thought about where to start.

"Think of a parent who brings a life into this world," the
doctor slowly began. "A 'bad' parent, if you will, would aban-
don that baby and not think twice about its welfare or education
or development, correct?"

The man and Faustina nodded in unison.

"Well, after my first five years of creating life and then abandoning my children—if you will—to the world, setting them adrift with their culture and history all wiped clean, I decided to violate the legal and ethical protocols and offer my reanimated subjects a little bit of their identity back when possible. Think about what I was struggling with. Yes, I did create life, but that life was a clean slate wiped of personal memories and experiences—all the things that make us who we are, the things that make us human. But I didn't want to do too much or leave my children's own desires and feelings out of the equation. So I settled on an elegant solution. I planted a hint, nothing more, in their belongings that they would eventually find. Perhaps a bit subtle, but I have found that it is just enough to allow my children's free will to take it from there and do what they need to do. For themselves, not for me."

"A hint?" said the man. "Like this children's book?"

"Yes, like that children's book, plus a note on my business card that left it to you when you were ready. That's called free will, no? And here you are, of your own volition. You must be ready. You have agency, as they say. And I am not the Dr. Frankenstein that so many people just love throwing at my face. Ni modo. That is a different discussion. In any event, I believe that I have answered the why. Now as for what the book means, are you ready for that?"

The man and Faustina looked at each other. Finally, the man turned back to the doctor and said softly, "Yes."

"There's a Mexican saying my mother used to rely on because, frankly, we didn't have much. She would say, 'A falta de pan, tortillas.' It's all about making do with what you've got. And for you, all I had was that children's book."

"How did you get it?" said Faustina.

"Another question!" said the doctor with a laugh. "But the answer to that helps me with responding to the question of what does it mean, no?"

"I suppose so," said the man.

"Are you sure you don't need a drink?" said the doctor.

Without waiting for a response, Faustina gave her drink to the man. The man looked at it, thought for a moment, took a gulp, then handed it back to Faustina.

"Wise move," said the doctor.

The man nodded, fortified by the alcohol.

"You died in a car crash," said the doctor. "The left side of your body was crushed, but the rest of you was almost pristine. Remarkable, really. I still have the photos at the lab. We photographed everything, but all of that is shut down, of course, and we are repurposing—as they say—our medical technology. We've learned a lot, you know. In any event, we were able to graft a new left arm and leg onto you. Sorry for not matching your left arm very well, but new limbs don't grow on trees, no pun intended. At least, we can't grow them yet!"

The doctor let out a guffaw at his last observation. The man and Faustina did not smile. The doctor composed himself and continued: "But when we put you together—me and my team— and completed the reanimation process, I thought you looked beautiful even with mismatched parts. Do you know why?"

The man shook his head.

"You were beautiful to me because you were alive," whispered the doctor.

"That's it?" said the man.

"What is more beautiful than life?"

The man and Faustina nodded in unison.

"In fact, when you first showed signs of life, I announced to my team: *He is alive!* Life is something that must be proclaimed, acknowledged, celebrated."

The room fell into silence as the man absorbed the doctor's observation.

"At the time of the crash," the doctor said as he finally finished his digression, "you had a box of belongings with you that included this children's book. There were other books but for adults as well, and some clothing, photographs, term papers, and the like. The best I could figure was that your mother had given you things that were cluttering up her home and that rightfully belonged with you—things that you had not taken earlier, when you had moved out on your own. Kids always do that. My son did, that's for sure. I still have a box or two of his stuff stored in the garage. Anyway, I kept your children's book and returned all of that other stuff to her."

"You mean, my mother?" said the man.

"Lo siento, I'm getting ahead of myself," said the doctor as he reached for the book again, opened it to the frontispiece, and pointed to the crayoned name. "This book belonged to a young boy named Fernando Ochoa."

"Me?" said the man.

"Yes."

Faustina handed her drink to the man, who took the glass and drained it.

"I know it's a lot," said the doctor.

"Why did you choose this one item for me?"

"Well," began the doctor, "childhood is an important time for our development as humans. Our brains are like sponges, absorbing language and sensations and, well, the world that will shape us into who we eventually become as adults. I made a calculated guess that the book was precious to your younger self—after all, why keep it as an adult? And so I slipped it into your belongings in that cardboard box when you were transferred to your transitional housing after reanimation. So in my mind, that book represented your childhood. ¿Entiendes?"

"I think so," said the man. "I think that makes sense."

"But why not give him more?" said Faustina. "Why play a *Citizen Kane* game with him?"

"Oh, I love that movie!" laughed the doctor. "Rosebud, am I right?"

"I don't know what that means," said the man.

"I'll tell you later," said Faustina. "And we'll stream the movie. You'll love it, I hope. If you don't, I might have to leave you."

"Ha!" laughed the doctor. "I like this woman. But back to your question. Why did I choose this book? I had to be careful about how much I could breach the protocols. They have eyes everywhere, you know. Sometimes it was easy to become quite paranoid. Even now, with reanimation shut down, there are search warrants and the like. So, you know, I risked my medical and reanimation licenses. I had to be subtle, not get too bold, avoid raising any red flags. Just enough not to be a superfluous man. But some of the protocols made sense. One of the key protocols is to protect the survivors, allow them to grieve the loss of a loved one, move on with their lives. Your former self— Fernando Ochoa—is essentially dead."

"But…" said the man.

"The person who was Fernando Ochoa," continued the doctor, "no longer exists and he can never be truly resurrected. Period. Fin de la historia. That's something you need to accept."

"What can you tell me about my mother?" said the man.

"Well, not much. Nothing more than her last address. But I can't give that to you, unless…"

"Unless what?" said the man.

"Again, as I said, you have to understand that some protocols should not be violated. You had signed a donor card where you agreed that upon reanimation, you'd be as good as dead to your family and friends. All of your old social media accounts were wiped and personal records purged. You got a new Social Security card and driver's license, both marked with a big red *R* on the front of them. A scarlet letter! Your reanimation credential replaced your old birth certificate. And if you ever had your DNA determined by one of those companies—Ancestry or 23andMe or whatever—the reanimation statute required them to block those records and prevent any future attempt by a reanimated subject from getting a DNA test. If you ever became famous, you couldn't be a guest of Henry Louis Gates Jr. on that PBS show, that's for sure."

"Oh, I love *Finding Your Roots*," said Faustina.

"Why go through so much trouble?" said the man.

"All of that protects your family and friends as much as it protects you," said the doctor before taking another drink. "I mean, you are not the same person they knew. It would be disastrous to pretend otherwise, no? But at the same time I understand your desire to know your roots. It's very normal. That's why you'd have to promise before I can give you any more information, such as your mother's address."

"Promise what?" said Faustina.

The man stared at the doctor and waited for an answer to Faustina's question.

"If I give you the address, you must promise me that you will not inform anyone from your prior life who you were. You are dead to them, so you must understand that they have already mourned your loss. You could cause great emotional damage if you're not careful. Can you imagine a situation, for example, where a reanimated subject returns to his former home and finds that his spouse has remarried and started a new life that might even include children? That kind of thing. People have moved on. And if they're healthy about such things, they've processed the loss in whatever stages work for them. You are nothing more than a memory. And your memory of your past life was wiped with the reanimation process. So they are really strangers to you, no matter how much you might want otherwise. You can't truly miss what you don't remember."

"But he could promise you anything to get that information and just lie through his teeth," said Faustina. "I mean, think about it. You're asking a lot. Maybe too much. He could lie to your face and you'd never know."

"True," said the doctor. "But not likely. One of things we've observed this last decade of reanimation is that our subjects are remarkably honest—honest to a fault, you might even say. Maybe it has to do with the wiping of their histories in the reanimation process."

"I knew you were different from all the other guys I dated," said Faustina with a laugh.

"Ha!" said the doctor. "That's a good one."

"Okay," said the man. "I promise."

The room grew quiet. The doctor nodded slowly.

"But if I give you the address," said the doctor, "I will also give you some background as well as a story that you can tell those you end up meeting. I know it will feel like a lie, but we will practice, and it will be for their—and your—protection. Are you okay with that?"

"Yes," said the man. "I am okay with that. I promise."

"And above all else, you must remember one thing," said the doctor.

"And what's that?" said the man.

"No matter what you learn about your former self, and no matter what cover story we come up with, the most important thing you must remember is that you are alive. Got that? Alive. In the here and now. What you are experiencing is real. It's just different from what you had before."

"Yes," said the man. "I am alive."

Faustina looked at the man and squeezed his right arm.

"Good," said the doctor. "We can get down to business."

"But," said the man, "what about these?" He withdrew from his shirt pocket a bottle of pills. "I am almost out. I can't find any more at the pharmacy. I've been cutting them in half."

"Those are worthless," the doctor laughed. "Just a simple antihistamine, nothing more."

"I was told that I had to take it or else I wouldn't live my full twenty years."

"Just another revenue stream for Big Pharma," said the doctor.

"But why would they do that?" said the man.

"Occam's razor."

"What?"

"The simplest explanation is preferable to one that is more complex," said the doctor. "Greed is the answer, pure and simple. It is the great motivator. So this alleged need for a reanimation medication was part of the backroom dealmaking that a few Senators got for their pharmaceutical donors. The circle of life… for the scum of the Earth."

"So I don't need my medication?"

"You will live as long as any person, so just eat your vegetables, exercise, floss your teeth, and love the one you're with, as the old song goes."

"Oh," said the man.

"That's fucked," said Faustina. "Not your health advice and loving the one you're with. The Big Pharma bullshit."

"Yes," said the doctor. "Royally fucked. Cabrones, all of them! It's emblematic of their thinking, you know that? Better to reign in hell than to serve in heaven, that's their motto. They don't mind being cast from heaven as long as their pockets are bulging with dinero. The almighty dollar is their god. And besides, they never viewed the reanimated community as being fully human anyway. Just some kind of... of... let me think, what's a good metaphor? Golem. That's it! Golem, not human."

"What's a 'golem'?" said the man.

The doctor thought for a moment, then scanned the room. He let out a little grunt when his eyes landed on a pile of books set atop the coffee table. The doctor stood and walked to the table, lifted three books, and snatched a fourth, then returned the first three with an alacrity that startled the man and Faustina. He handed the book to the man as if offering a rare, bejeweled gift.

"Read this when you have a chance," said the doctor. "Essentially, a golem is an artificial human being from Jewish folklore, but this book explains its rich history."

The man took the book from the doctor and read its title aloud: "*The Golem Redux: From Prague to Post-Holocaust Fiction.*"

"It's a fascinating book that will answer all your questions about all things golem," said the doctor. "In some ways I prefer the golem metaphor over some of the other ones like, you know, the Shelley novel. Though I sort of like the moniker of the 'modern Prometheus.' Nothing beats being a Titan unless, of course, your father is Zeus and decides to punish you. Then watch out for your liver!" said the doctor as he took another drink. "Though I'd love my liver to grow back each day."

"Poor old Prometheus," said Faustina with a laugh. The man blinked, not certain what to think.

"But I'm no Victor Frankenstein," continued the doctor. "And you are not a monster. You are a person. And every person has value, no? Frankly, the ones who call you a monster are the real monsters. Ni modo. We need to focus on the task at hand."

The man placed the golem book on the couch and waited.

The doctor walked to the bookshelves that covered the far wall. He scanned the titles, muttering to himself, and then said, "Ah!" He reached for a tattered paperback book and walked over to the man and Faustina.

"Let's begin with this," said the doctor as he presented the book to the man.

Quetzalcoatl looked up at the humans, licked its lips, and closed its eyes again. The man received the book and scanned its cover. He mouthed to himself, ". . . y no se lo tragó la tierra by Tomás Rivera."

"I read that novel in college," said Faustina. "The English translation, though. I love the title: … And the Earth Did Not Devour Him. I mean, how many book titles begin with an ellipsis? Those three little dots say so much. Anyway, after I read the English translation, I was able to make it through the original Spanish with the help of a dictionary. So beautiful."

"It's a bilingual edition," said the doctor. "The translation is actually quite good. The translator is a poet in her own right, so even the English sings!"

"Do you want me to read it?" asked the man.

"Only if you want to, later. But more importantly, you should open it," said the doctor as he walked to the turntable and flipped the Tierra album over. As the first song of side two started, the doctor closed his eyes and hummed a little to himself, lost in a faraway happy memory. He sighed, opened his eyes, and walked slowly back to the couple.

The man opened the book, and hidden in the pages was a folded piece of paper. He carefully pulled it out, handed the book to Faustina, and unfolded the paper.

"The FBI searched my hard drive and cell phone, but they were daunted by my thousands of books," said the doctor. "They never looked into any of the volumes on these two walls because they got tired of opening book after book after book on that smaller bookcase over there," he added with a chuckle as he pointed to a bulging bookcase near the fireplace. "I got the idea from an Edgar Allan Poe short story. Hidden in plain sight!"

The man studied the handwritten notes on the paper.

"It's just bare-bones information on you—who you were—like date of birth, schools you attended, what you studied in college, your most recent employment, et cetera," said the doctor. "You weren't married, and you didn't have any children."

"And this name here," said the man, "Elisa Ochoa, is that my mother?"

"Yes," said the doctor. "And that's her last known address. Right here in Oxnard. That's why I asked you to pack a few things when you first called me. You can stay in my guest room, not a problem. The foldout is actually quite comfy. I am a longtime widower, and my son is across the country teaching biology at Brown, so you won't be in the way. It'd be kind of nice to have people around this big house. I can cook a big breakfast. I was planning on chorizo con huevo, steaming corn tortillas, and gallons of coffee. But if you want, there's also a Comfort Inn, and I think a Hilton, and other hotels not too far from here if you prefer to have your own space, as they say. Ni modo. I thought that you might want to pay a visit tomorrow to Elisa Ochoa, since it's Sunday."

The man looked at Faustina, who shrugged.

"We can stay here tonight," said the man.

"And your suggested breakfast menu sounds better than anything I can think of," said Faustina. "Thank you!"

"Por nada," said the doctor. "And it will give us a bit more time to plot out a cover story for you. We don't want to upset anyone."

"Yes," said the man. "We don't want to upset anyone."

At that moment, Quetzalcoatl woke from its nap, blinked, yawned, and let out a small meow.

The doctor laughed. "The mention of chorizo con huevo must have broken into Quetzi's dreams. Let me feed my little friend first. Sadly, Quetzi will have to dine on more traditional cat food. Then we three can get down to work and get ready for your big visit tomorrow."

"Yes, I would like that," said the man.

"Sounds like a plan," said Faustina.

"Yes, it does," said the doctor as he reached down to pick up the cat. "Yes, it does."

ATTORNEY GENERAL LAUNCHES INDUSTRY INVESTIGATION OF REANIMATION PROTOCOL BREACHES

WASHINGTON (AP)—Attorney General Joyce McCluskie launched a formal, wide-ranging investigation Thursday into the reanimation industry for what she called "egregious" and "systematic" breaches of the so-called Stitcher Protocols that had been in place prior to President Mary Beth Cadwallader's recent banning of the reanimation procedure.

"One of the reasons the president outlawed reanimation was the brazen pattern and practice of protocol violations that undermined not only the rule of law but also the moral fiber of our society," said the attorney general, who was joined by her legal team at the press conference.

"Recent FBI raids uncovered extensive potential violations as well as potential coverups at the highest levels of some of our largest targets," said McCluskie. The attorney general declined to name which companies were targets, though one of the highest-profile FBI raids was conducted last month at Clerval Industries, based in Oxnard, California.

McCluskie, in rather vague terms, described the alleged protocol violations as being tied to actions by industry doctors to maintain contact with reanimated subjects in order to inculcate them with "politically correct" and "race-based" information of their prior lives.

When asked if the investigation was related to the upcoming midterm elections and the president's desire to maintain her majorities in both the House and Senate, the attorney general vehemently denied the accusation.

"We are about doing the right thing, uninfluenced by politics or party affiliation," said McCluskie. "We are the Department of Justice, not the department of midterms," she added with a chuckle.

McCluskie has been mentioned as a potential replacement for Supreme Court Associate Justice Alexander Williams, who turned 87 last week and has been in ill health since suffering a series of strokes at the end of last term. Justice Williams, however, has refused to step down and issued a statement last week indicating, in his trademark colorful language, a desire to continue working until he is "carried out of my chambers, boots first."

Chapter Twenty-Two

THE MAN CLOSED DR. Prietto's front door and entered the cool evening. The few sips of Faustina's drink had worn off after the two-hour prep session the doctor put him and Faustina through for tomorrow's visit. He looked down at the jack-o'-lantern that offered in response a silent maniacal scream. The man made a face back at the carved pumpkin and let out a small laugh. He stretched his legs and twirled his arms in three clockwise circles. The man took a deep breath, put on his hoodie, and then started on his run. He did not remember these Oxnard streets—the reanimation process wiped those memories away—but no matter. The man needed to feel his legs and arms work against the night in preparation for tomorrow. Despite some trepidation, a growing calm was beginning to bloom now that he had made it this far on his journey. And he had Faustina to thank for that. The full moon shone brightly as it lit the man's way down the unfamiliar street and seemed to warm his limbs with its glow.

When the man returned to Dr. Prietto's home after his run,

he took a long, hot shower and then snuggled behind Faustina in the guest bed. She stirred but did not wake. The man buried his face in the back of her neck and drifted to sleep within three minutes. The man fell into a dream, and it initially seemed to be the same dream he'd had each night since his reanimation. In the dream, faces—some familiar, some not—flickered and ebbed into view. Lips moved, words muttered, but the man could not discern their meaning. And then silence. Not a sound to be heard. Suddenly, the amorphous surroundings transformed into a beach, and the man found himself standing at the edge of the water. He looked down, and this is where his dream diverged from the other nights. A small boat floated on the water before him, but instead of carrying a body draped in a white shroud, there sat Faustina dressed in a flowing white dress. A voice commanded the man to step into the boat.

"Where are we going?" the man asked the disembodied voice.

"All will be revealed if you are ready to see," the voice answered.

And the man did what he was told. He settled in near Faustina, and the boat started to move forward of its own volition, the rippling water making a strange whispering sound.

As the boat steadily moved across what appeared to be an endless lake, the man forgot about Faustina sitting near him. His stomach rumbled and he allowed his mind to drift to imagined sumptuous meals that—unlike prior versions of this dream— he now had memories of consuming before. These foods were so wonderful, they filled him with great joy and warmth. The boat finally reached the other side of the lake. The man disembarked and then gave his hand to Faustina and helped her out of the boat and onto the warm sand. The man grew angry with himself because he had forgotten to ask the disembodied voice for further direction. But no matter. They would trudge forward. As they did, the man noticed that the terrain changed. Strange trees and plants sprouted from what was now a rocky, craggy ground. The man and Faustina marched a very long time, and they grew weary, each step becoming more and more difficult. The man's bare feet started to bleed as they were cut by the sharp, rocky ground. Faustina did not seem to encounter sharp rocks, and her steps remained light and unfettered by pain or discomfort, though she grew as weary as the man. The man eventually realized that the terrain had grown more fantastical with each step. Indeed, the shapes he saw seemed to become something more than terrain, something akin to a language. Not merely a language but a hieroglyph, ancient and mysterious, that spoke only to him. For some reason, Faustina did not understand what the shapes said, and she didn't seem to care. Without much effort, he deciphered the message. The man now knew what he needed to do and where they must go.

The man, armed with knowledge, finally reached the place where he could allow himself to rest and gather his wits. Faustina found a smooth boulder upon which to sit, and this gave the man great comfort. The man looked up and saw a large boulder shaped like a hand holding a ripe fig. The boulder balanced upon a pedestal of rock that jutted up from the sand. With an agility he did not possess while awake, the man scrambled up to the boulder and examined it. He placed his right hand on the boulder and the rock and felt the coolness of the stone. The man closed his eyes and offered a simple benediction for the emptiness he caressed: "May your history be complete." He removed his hand, nodded, and then scrambled back down.

After a few moments of silence, the man and Faustina

started their long trek back to the boat. They walked through the strange, craggy terrain, which eventually gave way to the gentle sand that they had first encountered. The sun warmed their bodies and the gentle sand seeped through their toes with each step. But their serenity was dashed when a group of dark figures without faces surrounded them. The man tried to scream but couldn't open his mouth. Faustina suddenly disappeared. These dark figures pulled at the man's arms—first his left, then his right—and bit his face and body as they snarled like rabid dogs. This torture went on and on and on. The only consolation the man felt was that Faustina was spared this fate because she was nowhere to be seen. Finally the dark figures dropped the man onto the ground and lurched away, muttering obscene sounds that were not quite words. The man lay bruised and bleeding, but in time he gathered himself up and stood. The man felt his body and confirmed that he was intact. And slowly he resumed his journey, limping in pain with each step. He wondered where Faustina was, but he could not bring himself to search. The man felt compelled to move forward.

The man made it to the boat, which seemed to be waiting for him. He got in, sat down, and closed his eyes. The man could feel the boat move, sliding slowly across the vast lake in the direction from where they had come. He eventually felt a presence near the boat, floating out before him in the water. The man's eyes popped open, and what he saw made him smile. A few yards from the boat's bow floated the dark figures that had accosted him previously. *There is justice*, thought the man. The boat slid by the bodies and the man grinned in satisfaction at the flotsam and jetsam that had been his tormentors.

In time the man's boat reached the shore. His bruises and lacerations had miraculously healed, and he felt fit and strong.

He closed his eyes to rest. When he opened them, Faustina sat next to him as she had when they first started their journey. Oh joy! The boat finally reached the shore, and the man stepped out of the boat first. He offered his right hand to Faustina, but at that moment, before she could grasp his hand, the man fell into darkness—fast and dizzying, deep, deep, deep into an abyss. Before the man hit the bottom, he awoke from his dream.

The man sat up and looked around room. At first he could not remember where he was, then he realized he was in the doctor's guest room. He saw Faustina on her side facing him, curled into a ball like a cat and snoring, face half buried in the man's pillow. The sheet had fallen to the floor, and the soft amber light of the nightstand lamp bathed Faustina in a gentle glow. The man softly touched Faustina's cheek. The man sighed, pulled the sheet around Faustina, snuggled into her, and fell into a dreamless sleep.

Chapter Twenty-Three

"ARE YOU READY?" SAID Faustina.

"Yes," said the man. "I think so."

They sat in Faustina's car; she had parked directly under an evergreen elm in front of a row of houses that were constructed immediately after World War II for the returning veterans who needed their piece of the American dream. But over the years the houses took on different colors of paint, and some were adorned with new windows and additions and a variety of landscaping such that their original sameness had all but vanished. The man and Faustina did not know any of this. All they knew was the address on the small brown house was the one given to them by the doctor. The midday sun warmed the inside of the car. They had wanted to get here earlier, but the doctor let them sleep late and then couldn't stop telling stories throughout their delicious breakfast.

"And you're comfortable with the cover story Dr. Prietto suggested?"

The man took a deep breath.

"Because if you're not," said Faustina, "we could leave right now and not do this. I know you don't like to lie."

"I can find truth in the cover story he suggested," said the man. "In some ways the cover story is truer than my own story—at least compared with the story of my current life."

"Okay, that works for me if it works for you. It's sort of like preparing a witness for deposition. Stick with what feels true because they'll know if you're lying."

The man unbuckled his seat belt and reached down to retrieve the cardboard box. He sat for a moment, listening to his own breathing. In, out; in, out; in, out. Long, controlled breaths to slow his heart, calm his nerves. Then slowly the man opened his door, got out, and stood under the tree. Faustina removed her car keys and joined the man on the grass by the curb. Clouds obscured the noonday sun. Faustina looped her left arm around the man's right, and the man held the cardboard box tightly to his chest with his left arm. They slowly started to walk toward the little brown house.

"We can still turn back," said Faustina.

"No," said the man.

They reached the front door. The man rang the doorbell, and they waited. After a few seconds, the door opened, but the metal screen door remained closed. A young woman stood in the doorway behind the safety of the screen.

"Yes?" said the young woman.

The man cleared his throat. "I—we—are looking for Elisa Ochoa," he said in a soft voice.

"That's me."

"Sorry?" said Faustina.

"I'm Elisa Ochoa," repeated the young woman. "What is this about?"

"I thought you'd be older," said the man.

"Oh, I'm sorry. I get it. I'm named after Mom."

"Ah," said Faustina.

"May we see her?" said the man. "I have something for her."

"Well," said Elisa. "That would be difficult."

"Is she away?" said the man.

"Mom passed two years ago."

A shock ran through the man's body. He shivered.

"We had something for her," said Faustina, pointing to the cardboard box, remembering the doctor's cover story. "Something that belonged to her son, Fernando."

"Oh!" said Elisa. "Did you two know my brother?"

"Yes," said the man, recovering his composure and remembering the general contours of the cover story. He told Elisa his name and introduced Faustina as his fiancée, just as they had agreed to do the night before at the doctor's home. "Fernando and I both studied for our paralegal certificates together. Anyway, I ended up with one of his books—I don't remember how—and I thought his mother would want it."

With that pronouncement, the man opened the cardboard box and pulled out the book. Elisa gasped. She quickly opened the screen door and ushered them in.

"That's where it went!" said Elisa. "We couldn't figure out what had happened to it, you know, after the accident. Mom thought that it had been in a larger box with Fernando's other things that she had given him that day. But I guess it wasn't. May I?"

The man handed the book to Elisa, who carefully opened it to its frontispiece. She softly outlined her brother's name with her right index finger. Elisa sighed.

"Please sit," she said gesturing toward a long couch. "Can I get you anything?"

"No, we're fine," said the man. "We had a big breakfast."

The man and Faustina got comfortable on the couch. Elisa sat in a nearby matching loveseat and continued to page through the book. The man looked about the room. It was comfortable, homey, lived in. His family was not rich, but they had enough money to be content in this well-kept, unostentatious house. The man turned his gaze back to his sister and waited for her to finish paging through the book.

"We were so proud of him," said Elisa when she got to the last page. "He was the first person in our family to go to college. Pop died when I was a baby. Lung cancer, probably from working in the strawberry fields with all of those pesticides. Mom's English was way better because she was born here in Oxnard. She worked for years as a secretary at Our Lady of Guadalupe Parish School. Anyway, they were so proud of Fernando when he graduated from San Diego State."

"Yes," said the man. "I can imagine."

"And then getting his paralegal credential, that was pretty amazing," continued Elisa. "Fernando said that if he could go to college, I could too, because I was smarter than him." She let out a little laugh. "I always thought that was funny, but hey, it worked. I graduate next year from Cal State Channel Islands."

"What do you study?" said the man.

"Applied physics."

"Wow," said Faustina. "A woman in STEM. Excellent!"

"Fernando was always impressed by that too," said Elisa. "He said science wasn't his thing, and he didn't get it. But he loved history and did really well in it at college. That was his major, actually. American history with a minor in Latin American history."

"History," murmured the man as he let the thought roll around in his mind. "History."

Elisa smiled. She looked at the book again and thought for a moment.

"I know what to do with this," she finally said.

Elisa stood and walked to the far end of the room. In the corner by the brick fireplace stood a small table draped in a very worn multicolored serape. The tabletop was adorned with marigolds in a glass vase, two colorful sugar skulls, a plate of pan dulce, a small pitcher of water, two lit votive candles emblazoned with images of the Virgin of Guadalupe, and a cluster of burning sticks of incense protruding from a small ceramic skull. The man and Faustina stood and followed Elisa. And it was then that they noticed two framed photographs positioned side by side at the back of the table, one of an older woman and one of a young man. Four smaller framed photographs of these same people as teenagers and young children were arranged at the foot of the two larger photographs. A large framed photograph of an older man stood watch over the others.

"Perfect timing for Día de los Muertos," said Elisa as she set the book on the ofrenda. "Fernando will be happy to find his favorite childhood book."

The man and Faustina came closer to the little altar. The candles seemed to flicker and dance as they drew near. They stood in silence with Elisa and admired the beautiful ofrenda.

"Who is that?" asked the man, pointing to the photograph of the older man.

"That's Pops," said Elisa. "He passed when I was a baby."

"Oh," said the man. He sighed.

"I know you said you had a big breakfast, but I'd love for you to stay for lunch," said Elisa after a few moments. "I'm doing a nice salad, so it won't be too heavy."

The man looked a Faustina, searching for an answer. She

shrugged. This was clearly his decision. The man turned back to Elisa.

"Yes," said the man.

"We'd be honored," said Faustina.

"Good! I want to talk about my brother," said Elisa. "Ever since Mom was called back, it's been just me in this house with a lot of memories. It will be nice to talk to someone who knew Fernando. I miss him so much."

"So do I," said the man. "So do I."

"Have we," began Elisa as she stared intently at the man, "ever met? Maybe at Fernando's graduation? Or the memorial service?"

"That wasn't me," said the man, attempting to cling as close to the truth as possible but eventually not knowing what was true and what was not. "I couldn't walk at graduation because of a family medical situation. And I was out of the country during his memorial service."

"Oh," said Elisa. "I was sure we'd met before."

FAUSTINA EASED HER CAR onto the 101. Traffic was lighter than yesterday when they drove to Oxnard from Pasadena. At least their drive home would not be as long. The man stared ahead at the other cars. His stomach was full of wonderful food, and his head swam with Elisa's stories about Fernando. The man ended up not saying very much, just listening to his sister go on and on about the person he used to be. And he liked what he heard. Fernando was a kind person, someone who worked hard and took care of his mother and sister. Fernando also had a little trouble maintaining relationships—not because he was mean-spirited, just a little insecure and a bit shy. At least that's how Elisa saw it. The man laughed softly.

"What's so funny?" said Faustina.

"Well," began the man, "I think I would have liked myself."

Faustina nodded, hesitated, then decided not to say anything. They drove in silence all the way back to Pasadena.

PARTIAL TRANSCRIPT OF MSNBC ELECTION NIGHT

WITH JOY REID, ARI MELBER, AND STEVE KORNACKI

MELBER: And we're back from our short break, bringing you election night coverage. Turning back to what Joy was saying before the commercial, pollsters must be feeling pretty embarrassed tonight as we watch these numbers come in. The midterms are not turning out as they predicted.

REID: I'm just saying, you know? We all listened to this narrative about a wave midterm, but they were dead wrong. I mean way dead and way wrong!

MELBER: Yep. That's for sure. And I think Steve Kornacki has some new numbers for us over at the Big Wall. Steve? What's getting you so excited over there? Something happening?

KORNACKI: Yes, well, the numbers from Arizona, Nevada, and New Mexico are coming in—we just got a huge dump in all three of those western states—so it might not be a late night if the numbers keep coming in this way.

REID: And from what I can see from here, it looks like folks at the White House proba-bly aren't too happy right now. They were banking on a wave election, but it looks like a ripple or worse.

KORNACKI: Right! Look at this one Arizona district right here. Let me move this and expand that. Oops! Let me try that again. Live TV, right? Okay, got it, this worked, and look: in the last count before the latest dump, the president's endorsed candidate for this House seat was ahead of her challenger by about three percentage points, but watch this, as we add those new numbers. Do you see that?

REID: Oh my! Look at that!

KORNACKI: The lead flipped completely. Wow, these numbers are really coming in, and clearly the early vote—which is tabulated after the same-day vote, obviously—is not going for the president's party. This is true in Nevada and New Mexico, too, if you look at these returns here and here. All three pivotal western states seem to be in lock-step not only for the House seats but also, look here, for the Senate as well. In fact, if trends continue as they are going now, the president will lose all three Senate seats that were up for election in these three states for this cycle. Not good, since the polls had indicated a midterm that defied history and would have allowed the president to keep or maybe even expand her majorities in both the House and Senate.

MELBER: Which, if things continue the way they are now, could completely block not only the president's legislative agenda but also any potential nominees to the federal bench, not to mention the Supreme Court if there's a vacancy in the next two years. The president will be rendered the lamest of ducks.

REID: Really quickly, Steve, just a quick follow-up, because President Cadwallader had been selecting and endorsing and even campaigning with candidates in her party's primaries who I think most objective observers would say are probably the weaker choice for her party in states like Nevada, Arizona, and New Mexico. You know, in the state of Arizona, is there a sense of how pro-Cadwallader the electorate is? Because, in some of these other swing states, the chances of the opposition party prevailing are actually being increased by Cadwallader's picks becoming the nominees.

KORNACKI: Yes. Well, like I said earlier, in Arizona there was a full six-point margin for Cadwallader two years ago, and she carried the state four years prior to that, though by only two points. So yes, many thought it was a safe state for the president's party. But now, look at this, even in the suburbs where the president had done so well, the margins are almost flipped in district after district.

This is a sea change, really. Something you don't see very often. And really a surprise, since the president's approval ratings are actually quite strong—historically speaking—and the polling in these three states looked pretty good for her handpicked candidates going into this night.

MELBER: But lest we forget, the president's anti-reanimation crusade—if I may use that word here—may have backfired, based on the exit polls we looked at a little while ago.

REID: Right, the western states include some of the largest reanimated communities, just looking at population and voting patterns. Everyone thought the president's Make America Safe Again campaign was a winner—and the polls seemed to bear that out—but you know what? The only poll that counts is on election night, am I right? It's an old saying, but it's true.

MELBER: Yes! That's precisely what I'm thinking. The reanimated communities have been organizing and registering to vote at relatively higher numbers as compared with the president's core voting bloc. And I think the pollsters may have missed them or undercounted them so the polls didn't pick them up. And Steve's Big Board is showing that without a doubt.

REID: Steve Kornacki, you're the best. Thank you

	very much. We really appreciate you. And Steve will be at the Big Board throughout the night with results from today's mid-terms, which just keep on rolling in. We will definitely be keeping up with those numbers from key races.
MELBER:	Yes, Steve is the best!
KORNACKI:	Well, we have a lot of people helping make this all work. I'm just the messenger.
REID:	And so modest too! But yes, it's true we have a lot of great people working to make tonight possible.
MELBER:	And the other thing that's true is that we need to take another break. We'll be back after this message with all the numbers on this exciting election night and more Steve Kornacki at the Big Board. And it looks like we might have a new call from the decision desk when we come back.
KORNACKI:	They are working on it now, crunching numbers, seeing what the probabilities are based on what's left to count. Looks like we might have a big call in a minute or so on one or even two of the key races tonight.
REID:	Yeah, Kornacki! I could watch him all night. Especially with some of these races already getting defined much earlier than expected. But we can't count our chick-ens—am I right?—we need to see what the people are saying, not the polls or pundits like us, right?

MELBER: Yes, totally right. Let's see how all of this shakes out. And we will be right back after this quick message from the sponsors who keep our lights on.

REID: And the Big Board lit up!

MELBER: Yes, we can't forget the Big Board. Be right back after a couple commercials, folks. Much more to come on this exciting night.

—END OF TRANSCRIPT—

Chapter Twenty-Four

THE MAN SAT ALONE at his kitchen island. Today he did not need to go into the office, so he wore a faded blue polo shirt, Levi's, and flip-flops. He looked down at two pieces of pan dulce that sat on a plate—one with pink sugar topping, the other white. A steaming mug of coffee sat near the plate. The man breathed in the aroma of his breakfast and attempted to affix a word to what he felt at that moment. The morning sun was dulled by the dark clouds that threatened rain, so the man had turned on all of the kitchen's overhead lights, which illuminated his breakfast like searchlights scanning for survivors at sea. He considered his breakfast.

What do I want?

That was the question he now asked himself. The man knew he should want something as he looked upon his morning meal, a meal that had recently changed from his usual buttered wheat toast.

What do I want?

The man sensed something watching him. He turned his head toward the kitchen window and squinted. *Ah!* The neighbor's cat, Nacho, sat across his complex's communal backyard on the low retaining wall and stared at him. His friend, a tiger-striped feline. Nacho blinked, licked its lips, paused, blinked again, and scurried away. The man turned back to his breakfast and placed both hands, palms down, on either side of his plate. The cool white quartz felt solid, secure on his skin. He reformulated his question.

Whom do I want?

The man then focused on the contours of his hands. They remained dissimilar from each other, of course. Different sizes, different colors. These facts would not change, unlike his breakfast. Unlike the rest of his life. And then an answer came to him.

I want Faustina.

Faustina did not mind his patchwork body. Sometimes the man caught her staring at his hands, not in a cruel or judgmental manner but in a kind, gentle, thoughtful way. And so another question came to him.

What does Faustina want?

The man reached for the conchas, hesitated, thought about whether he should choose the pink one or the white one. His right hand hovered over the pan dulce.

"Chose one and leave the other for me, guapo."

The man turned and watched Faustina walk behind the island, open a cabinet, retrieve a coffee mug, and pour herself a cup. She turned toward the man.

"Any half-and-half left?"

Before the man could respond, Faustina opened the refrigerator, scanned its contents, and emitted a pleased *yes!* before retrieving a small carton.

"You're a bit low," said Faustina. "You might want to add it to your list."

After Faustina lightened her coffee to the appropriate shade of brown, she returned the carton to the refrigerator, walked around the edge of the island, and plopped down on the stool next to the man.

"I used my own deodorant and shampoo this time, guapo."

"Oh?" said the man.

"No more Irish Spring for me. That's your scent. I have stocked your medicine cabinet with some of my products as you suggested. Even some feminine hygiene items. Get used to it, pal! But I proceeded based upon your suggestion after all, right? And it was a thoughtful suggestion at that, guapo."

"Yes, it was."

Faustina laughed. "And thank you for buying a hair dryer," she added with a dramatic shake of her head that made her hair take up a great deal of airspace. "I look simply fabulous now."

The man noticed the woman's thick, curly, black hair bounce lightly. The woman smelled like her own shampoo mixed with her usual perfume. He admired how Faustina could look so beautiful wearing something as simple as a white T-shirt, jeans, and white canvas sneakers.

"You are beautiful," said the man. "I like looking at you."

"You charmer, you."

"I mean it. You are beautiful."

"And so are you."

The man blushed.

"Pink or white?" said Faustina.

"I don't know," said the man. "I can't seem to make a decision. Having wheat toast made my choices simpler."

"Simpler is not always better."

"That is true."

"How about I choose first, then?"

"Sí. You choose first. That will make it easier for me."

"I choose the pink," said Faustina as she reached for the pan dulce. "In honor of my inner Barbie."

"Sí," said the man. He smiled.

"And so you get what's left, guapo."

"Sí."

Faustina took a bite out of her concha. A shower of pink sugar fell onto her lap. Pink granules covered her lips. She laughed, shrugged, and took a long drink of her coffee. The man smiled, grabbed his napkin, and wiped Faustina's mouth.

"Such a gentleman," she said.

The man picked up the white concha, held it before his mouth for three seconds, and then bit in. A small smile appeared, and he nodded his approval. A memory tried to creep into his mind, but it quickly evaporated as the actual texture and flavor of the pan dulce took over.

"And next time," said Faustina, "when you stay over at my place, I will have cheese blintzes in honor of my Jewish stepfather."

"Sí. I would like that. I don't think I've ever had one before."

"As long as you keep on making good coffee, guapo, we have a deal."

"Gracias," said the man.

After a moment of quietly eating together, Faustina said, "Have you done the Wordle yet?"

"Not yet."

"I got it in three."

"You always beat me."

"Because I am very good with words, guapo," said Faustina.

"Though sometimes I try to use Spanish words that would fit perfectly, but they are rejected by the Wordle gods."

"I will do it later when I'm more awake."

"I did it half asleep, before my coffee."

"That way the odds are more even," said the man.

Faustina nodded and took a long drink of her coffee. They finished their breakfast in silence. Faustina then stood, put her coffee mug in the sink, walked back to the man, and pecked him on his left cheek.

"I've got to visit Mom and Saul," said Faustina. "They need some help with their computer."

"Puedo visitar más tarde," said the man. "I have to run by the market and get a few things first and then do two other errands."

"So organized," said Faustina. "Come by and visit when you're done. Mom and Saul would appreciate that. You know, they kind of like you."

"I like them. And I know it makes them happy to see us together."

"Thank you for being thoughtful."

"Por nada."

Faustina grabbed her purse and car keys from the end of the island and kissed the man one more time on the cheek. The man turned to Faustina, smiled, and kissed her lips. She kissed back, long and slow. Finally, Faustina pulled back and stroked the man's cheek.

"How about takeout from Urbano Mexican Kitchen tonight?" said Faustina after a thoughtful moment. "I love their carne asada burrito."

"Sounds good to me," said the man as he took in Faustina's scent with a deep breath. "Or maybe tacos from Guisados?"

"¡Ay, guapo! Why do you suggest an equally perfect option?"

"Lo siento."

"You're turning me into Buridan's ass! I'll starve before I can choose."

"Whose ass?"

"I'll explain later," said Faustina. "I have to run."

"I know you do."

Faustina sighed, turned, then left the apartment. In the silence of the kitchen the man thought about this woman who had just left. He could still feel her on his lips.

Faustina Godínez.

The man said Faustina's name aloud.

Faustina Godínez.

The man would never forget her name, unless he wanted to. But he doubted he would ever want to.

Faustina Godínez.

The man smiled. He looked at the two books on the kitchen island that the doctor had given him in Oxnard the week before. He reached for Tomás Rivera's … *y no se lo tragó la tierra*. He opened it to where he had placed a bookmark and started reading. After a few moments, he sensed that he was being watched again. The man turned toward the window and squinted. And there sat Nacho, sitting upright on the retaining wall and gazing back at him. They locked eyes for a long moment. The man finally let out a small, almost indecipherable laugh as he returned to his book.

After reading for a half hour, the man carefully set a bookmark where he had stopped and thought for a moment. He rubbed the stubble on his chin. Should he shave now or wait until later? Or perhaps not shave at all today, because it was, after all, the weekend, and he could give his face a rest from his usual fastidiousness. The man was in control of his time. There was no reason to do as he had planned. He was free to scrap that plan and start anew. Those errands could wait. He stood, stretched, paused for a moment, then walked slowly to his bedroom and changed into running clothes.

MEMORANDUM OF TELEPHONE CONVERSATION[1]

SUBJECT: Telephone Conversation with Vice President Martin Krempe

PARTICIPANTS: President Mary Beth Cadwallader
Vice President Martin Krempe
Notetakers: the White House Situation Room

DATE, TIME: November 10, 9:05–9:23 a.m. EDT

PLACE: Residence

POTUS: How is Germany going?

VPOTUS: Going well, I think. I can brief you more fully later on the whole military situation. I have several more meetings. The Germans want more support—you know—things are tense, so . . .

POTUS: It can wait. I've got the elections on my mind. We got fucked royally.

VPOTUS: I wish I could have been here for the midterms. I could have done something more to help.

POTUS: No, you did quite enough.

VPOTUS: [INAUDIBLE]

---

1 CAUTION: A memorandum of a Telephone Conversation (TELCOM) is not a verbatim transcript of a discussion. The text in this document records the notes and recollections of situation room duty officers and NSC policy staff assigned to listen and memorialize the conversation in written form as the conversation takes place. A number of factors can affect the accuracy of the record, including poor telecommunications connections and variations in accent and/or interpretation. The word inaudible is used to indicate portions of a conversation that the notetaker was unable to hear.

POTUS: No, I mean it. Not certain what the fuck more any of us could have done. Have you seen the numbers? They're still counting the mail-in vote, but it looks like those fucking stitchers came out in droves to vote against my candidates. Fuckers.

VPOTUS: I know. I saw the breakdown on MSNBC.

POTUS: Why the fuck are you watching MSNBC?

VPOTUS: I just like that Kornacki guy with his Big Wall. I tune out the rest.

POTUS: Everyone loves his fucking Big Wall.

VPOTUS: But the numbers . . .

POTUS: Yeah, the numbers were brutal.

VPOTUS: The reanimated turnout sort of got me thinking . . .

POTUS: By the way, you've really gotten control of that stutter of yours. I'm impressed.

VPOTUS: Been working on it, thank you. Plus this is a one-on-one conversation, so I'm more relaxed.

POTUS: Maybe we could use you more often . . .

VPOTUS: Anyway, the way Kornacki broke down the numbers, it got me thinking . . .

POTUS: [INAUDIBLE]

VPOTUS: Ha, ha. Right. Well, it got me thinking that if we removed the reanimated vote from the equation, we would have had a pretty good night.

POTUS: Too late for that. And you will be facing the same thing two years from now in the general election, if you can nail down the nomination. Maybe you need to start dusting off your resume.

VPOTUS: But that's the point.

POTUS: What's the point? You looking for a new gig?

VPOTUS: No, no. We've learned something from the midterms. If we can remove the reanimated vote from the equation, we should be fine in two years.

POTUS: What, you want to round them up and put them in camps or something?

VPOTUS: Well, that's one option.

POTUS: Hold on, what are you saying?

VPOTUS: Look, you have a lock—or a near lock—on the Supreme Court. So any executive order you issue should survive a legal challenge, right?

POTUS: Go on . . . I like what I'm hearing.

VPOTUS: Reanimation has already been outlawed, so the next logical step is to make reanimated subjects illegal as well.

POTUS: Right . . .

VPOTUS: And if they're illegal, what rights do they have? Not many, if you ask me.

POTUS: Go on . . .

VPOTUS: So maybe in the next few months, we—er, you—can start signing executive orders, each one tightening the noose.

POTUS: I get it . . .

VPOTUS: You know, the first order could limit their right to travel and hold certain jobs. Then maybe the next order could prohibit any intermarriage between the reanimated and normal people. And another order could close the borders to the reanimated from other countries.

POTUS: Yes! Shut those fucking stitchers down!

VPOTUS: Then the logical step would be to segregate them in facilities so we can keep track of them better until we can figure out the next steps. And then . . .

POTUS: And then?

VPOTUS: We use the final executive order to take away their vote.

POTUS: Yes!

VPOTUS: But it needs to be step-by-step.

POTUS: Inch by inch.

VPOTUS: Incremental.

POTUS: Slow drip.

VPOTUS: But not too slow.

POTUS: Boy, you finally impressed me.

VPOTUS: Thank you.

POTUS: This could work, you know that?

VPOTUS: It could, but we won't know unless we try.

POTUS: Oh, and you're a philosopher, too, now. You must be getting laid in Germany or something.

VPOTUS: Barbara is with me. It's our twenty-fifth wedding anniversary, actually.

POTUS: So you definitely aren't getting laid. Okay, maybe it was the schnitzel that shot a rocket up your ass and got you thinking

	like a real pro. Who knows. Whatever it was, you've put your motherfucking thinking cap on this time.
VPOTUS:	Well, I was elected to the Senate twice, so I guess I have a little . . .
POTUS:	I want you to head up the team to start drafting these fucking executive orders.
VPOTUS:	I would be honored. It's the American thing to do.
POTUS:	I have a breakfast with the goddamn Mexican ambassador in five minutes. The only good thing about that is we're having huevos rancheros. Love their food, hate their country. Let's circle back later.
VPOTUS:	Yes.
POTUS:	And you know what?
VPOTUS:	What?
POTUS:	You weren't a mistake after all.
VPOTUS:	Ha! Thank you, Madam President. That means a lot coming from you.
POTUS:	And so it should. And so it should.

—END OF CONVERSATION—

Chapter Twenty-Five

THE MAN WALKED OUT of his apartment, closed the door, and entered the cool morning. He examined the gray clouds that obstructed the sun and cast a dull shadow on the neighborhood. But the clouds passed quickly and the morning brightened. He stretched his legs and twirled his arms in three clockwise circles. He took a deep breath, put on his hoodie, and then started on his run. The man turned left on Hurlbut Street toward Pasadena Avenue and then stopped. He normally turned left, but today he would do something different, so he turned right. He let his legs stretch out in long strides as his muscles slowly warmed up. His arms and legs moved as they should, as a whole, constructed as perfectly as an antique pocket watch but with slightly mismatched, salvaged parts. But those parts all fit in their own peculiar way. The man's breathing grew heavy as his legs moved faster and faster in the cool morning. His mind was free and clear as he ran and ran and ran.

Acknowledgments

AS I HAVE ADMITTED on many occasions, giving thanks is fraught with peril because it is impossible to list every person who played a role in the creation of a book. But I will attempt this impossible task—perhaps as a modern-day Sisyphus—so please forgive me if your name does not appear here; you know who you are, and I am deeply indebted to you.

A big Chicano abrazo to my publisher, Laura Stanfill, founder of Forest Avenue Press. Your enthusiasm for and understanding of my novel is all that an author could ever desire. I thank you with all of my heart.

Many thanks to those passionate, brilliant editors of the magazines, newspapers, presses, literary journals, and anthologies who have either published me or given my work coverage over the years. Writing is a lonely business often filled with disappointment and hurdles, so your support has encouraged me to keep on going despite that small nagging voice of doubt that creeps into my mind late at night when my defenses are down.

I want to give another big Chicano abrazo to the many talented and unfaltering writers who have encouraged and inspired my literary life. Listing their names would require a whole book unto itself. And as I have done so often before, I offer additional thanks to my fellow bloggers at the online literary site *La Bloga*: You never fail to offer communal support for our strange vocation.

As for my day job, I offer thanks to my friends at the California Department of Justice who have read my books and attended my various virtual and in-person book readings. You continue to help me balance my life as a lawyer with that of an author.

I thank my parents, who always made certain that we were a family of books and that we freely used our library cards. You taught your children to love and appreciate reading, the arts, and our culture. Pop, though you have left this physical world, I know you are with me every day. I also know that you wanted to be a published writer as a young man, but back in the late 1950s and early 1960s, publishers were much less open to Chicano writers than they are now. So the pride you showed when I published my first book almost twenty-five years ago meant so much to me. I love and miss you, Pop. And Mom, your unfaltering love and support have made me the man I am today. And your wonderful family stories have enriched your children by reminding us of our Mexican roots and culture. You will see some of those stories reflected in this, my latest book.

Finally, I thank my wife, Susan Formaker, and our son, Benjamin Formaker-Olivas. As I have said before, I am nothing without you. I hope that you enjoy my new book. It is imbued with your love and support.

Source Acknowledgments

CHAPTER ELEVEN IS ADAPTED from the short story "The Last Dream of Pánfilo Velasco" first published in *Fairy Tale Review* (2014) and featured in *The King of Lighting Fixtures: Stories* (University of Arizona Press, 2017). © 2014 by Daniel A. Olivas. Reprinted by permission of the author.

"THE STORY OF FERNANDO" in Chapter Fourteen was first published in serialized form in the *Los Angeles Times* (2003). © 2003 by Daniel A. Olivas. Reprinted by permission of the author.

EXCERPTS OF *CHICANO FRANKENSTEIN* appeared in the *Boston Review* (2023).

About the Author

DANIEL A. OLIVAS, THE grandson of Mexican immigrants, was born and raised near downtown Los Angeles. He is an award-winning author of fiction, nonfiction, plays, and poetry, including *My Chicano Heart: New and Collected Stories of Love and Other Transgressions* (University of Nevada Press), *How to Date a Flying Mexican: New and Collected Stories* (University of Nevada Press), and *Things We Do Not Talk About: Exploring Latino/a Literature through Essays and Interviews* (San Diego State University Press). Olivas co-edited *The Coiled Serpent: Poets Arising from the Cultural Quakes and Shifts of Los Angeles* (Tía Chucha Press), and edited *Latinos in Lotusland: An Anthology of Contemporary Southern California Literature* (Bilingual Press). Widely anthologized, he has written on culture and literature for *The New York Times*, *Los Angeles Review of Books*, *Los Angeles Times*, *Alta Journal*, *Jewish Journal*, *Zócalo*, *Latino Book Review*, and *The Guardian*. He writes regularly for *La Bloga*, a site dedicated to Latinx literature and the arts. Olivas received his degree in English literature from Stanford University and his law degree from UCLA. By day, Olivas is an attorney and makes his home in Southern California with his wife (and law school sweetheart), Susan Formaker, who is an administrative law judge. They have an adult son, Ben Formaker-Olivas, who is a graduate of UCLA and works in the video game design industry.

CHICANO FRANKENSTEIN

DANIEL A. OLIVAS

READERS' GUIDE

Author's Note:
The Monster Within Us

As WITH MOST ADULTS born during the last century, my first exposure to Mary Wollstonecraft Shelley's *Frankenstein; or, The Modern Prometheus* was not through her genre-defining novel but by way of the 1931 classic black-and-white Universal Pictures film directed by James Whale and starring Boris Karloff as the monster. That celluloid creature imprinted itself on my five-year-old psyche like no other movie horror of my 1960s childhood.

And as is common with children—and not a few adults—I erroneously referred to the monster by the name that belonged to his obsessed creator, a doctor who dared play God. But no matter. I was mad about Frankenstein! I even successfully pleaded with my parents for a mechanical, battery-operated, green, flat-topped monster whose arms would rise up as if to grab me as he shuffled around emitting an eerie metallic groan. It was one of my favorite birthday gifts ever.

Of course, I knew nothing of the Greek immigrant, Jack Pierce (born Yiannis Pikoulas), who created the original iconic monster makeup for Karloff. Indeed, I didn't even know that I was watching an actor in disguise. At that age, it was all real to me, even as my parents calmed me with the words, "Don't be scared. It's only a movie."

Only a movie! Yeah, right. But I couldn't stop watching even as I was frightened beyond anything I had experienced up to that point in my young life. (Little did I know that the monsters of adulthood would be scarier than anything I could then imagine.) I even reveled in other movie versions of my favorite monster, including the horror-comedy *Abbott and Costello Meet Frankenstein* with the great Bela Lugosi as Count Dracula, who is in search of a "pliable" brain to reactivate the monster (gamely played this time by Glenn Strange). For good measure, the movie includes a subplot involving the Wolf Man, played by Lon Chaney Jr. Watching this film on our family's black-and-white television set may have been my first experience being both frightened and tickled silly at the same time.

About a decade later—sometime in high school—I finally read the Shelley novel, and I was shocked to learn that the monster actually remains nameless throughout the book. And not only that, he learns to read and eventually speak rather eloquently, unlike the grunting, monosyllabic creature of the movies. But I found it impossible not to envision Karloff in full makeup as I read the book that truly brought the monster to life.

Little did I know that the conflation of the monster and his creator—as well as his appearance as a hulking, green creature—grew out of the imaginations of English and French playwrights who adapted the novel for the stage in the decades after the 1818 publication of *Frankenstein*. As Professor Eileen

Hunt Botting (who now goes by Eileen M. Hunt) observes in her well-researched and engrossing book *Artificial Life After Frankenstein*, those plays influenced English playwright Peggy Webling's late 1920s stage adaptation, where she names the creature after his creator. And in the 1931 script Webling collaborated with John Balderston and added intriguing changes, including the monster's donning of Dr. Frankenstein's clothing. As Hunt observes: "This conflation of father and son still dominates popular culture to the point that most readers of the original novel are surprised to learn that Shelley left the Creature nameless." It is this Webling-Balderston script that Universal Studios relied upon to produce what Hunt calls the "most influential cinematic adaptation of the novel to date."

But in both the original Shelley novel and the adaptations that followed, one plot point remained more or less the same: Dr. Frankenstein's creature is eventually shunned by both his creator and society as a monster. And it is this rejection that turns the creature into a murderous revenge machine. Indeed, in the novel, the creature exclaims: "I am malicious because I am miserable. Am I not shunned and hated by all mankind?"

Fast-forward almost sixty years, and the little boy who developed a love-hate relationship with that green monster has written a novel inspired by Shelley's two-century-old tale. On October 10, 2022, I started writing *Chicano Frankenstein* and finished it November 29. While this may sound somewhat fast, I had been thinking about it for over a year, during which time I listened to a free audiobook of *Frankenstein* several times to refresh my memory of the story arc and to fuel my inspiration. I immediately came up with a title that would eventually become permanent. I mentally plotted my story and worked through tough narrative knots on my lunchtime walks. Because of my day job as a government attorney, I relegated myself to writing early in the morning and after dinner. I used whatever free time I had on weekends and the Thanksgiving holiday to make a great deal of headway. After Forest Avenue Press acquired my novel in spring 2023, I made a few edits and even added a reference to Hunt's *Artificial Life After Frankenstein*, which I read after my manuscript had been accepted for publication.

Those were the mechanics of writing *Chicano Frankenstein*. But why did I feel compelled to write it?

For twenty-five years, my fiction, poetry, and plays have been deeply rooted in my Mexican and Chicano culture. I have never limited myself to one way of exploring my community in literature. I love writing in many genres: social realism, magical realism, science fiction, noir, fabulism, horror, and everything in between. I see no reason to tie myself down to merely one type of storytelling. That would be quite boring, and the last thing I want to do is bore myself. Moreover, I am often inspired by other storytellers and how they express themselves. Since I read widely, I am inspired by a myriad of genres. It was inevitable that I would eventually return to my childhood's favorite monster for literary inspiration. And the more I thought about it, there was something about Shelley's tale that seemed perfectly situated to offer a springboard for many of the social and political issues I had been thinking about in fall of 2022.

And what were those issues? The midterm election cycle brought another round of angry MAGA candidates who continued to promote the Trumpian lie of a stolen 2020 election. Part and parcel of their rhetoric was—yet again—an attack on immigrants and anyone who just didn't fit in with their image of "real" Americans. For my novel, I decided to create a similar midterm election in an alternative near future, and

I would intersperse my narrative with news reports, political commercials, talking heads on cable shows, and Oval Office meeting transcripts.

As for the "monster" of my story, I created a world very much like our own, but where reanimation of the recently deceased—though otherwise healthy adults—had been perfected as a way to replenish an aging workforce. After a decade's worth of reanimation, twelve million so-called "stitchers" (a cruel epithet) now walked among us in the United States. The hero of my tale is an unnamed paralegal who was brought back to life through this controversial process. We watch him maneuver through a world that both needs and resents him. A foulmouthed President Mary Beth Cadwallader spouts toxic anti-reanimation rhetoric to goose her midterm numbers in the House and Senate races. All the while, my unnamed man falls in love with a lawyer, Faustina Godínez. Quite naturally, this relationship expands his world as he meets Faustina's network of family and friends, setting him on a journey to find the doctor who reanimated him so that the man can discover his first-life history, which the reanimation process erased.

My novel is not a mirror image of Shelley's, but that's how inspiration works. And the fact that a Chicano writer, two hundred years after the publication of *Frankenstein*, could draw inspiration from Shelley's narrative to create something new points to the brilliance of her storytelling. Shelley created a world that is so rich and complex that hundreds if not thousands of other novelists, playwrights, filmmakers, animators, and graphic artists have been as inspired as I have to create their own version of *Frankenstein*. Some have explored the parent-child relationship between Dr. Victor Frankenstein and his creation, as did Mel Brooks and Gene Wilder in their wonderfully off-kilter 1974 comedy, *Young Frankenstein*. Others—like me— focus on what we consider the inherently political implications of being a "monster" in a society that created you on the one hand and is repulsed by you on the other.

In the end, many critics believe the remarkable legacy of Shelley's *Frankenstein* goes beyond the creation of a horrifying tale. Her story forces us to ask difficult questions about human nature, abusive relationships, and science gone awry. And for some readers—such as myself—Shelley's novel shines a bright light on the usually irrational fear of "the other" (to use a contemporary term). This particular take on *Frankenstein* raises the ultimate question: Who is the real monster among us? Put another way, what person is truly free from bias? Even the most open-minded person carries decades of implicit bias accumulated from a myriad of environments: home, work, and society in general. It takes great effort to truly see a person's full worth without reservation. So, regrettably, I suspect that the monster may very well be within each of us.

Reading List: Books Mentioned in Daniel A. Olivas's Novel

HERE ARE THE BOOKS the author included in the text of *Chicano Frankenstein*:

Elizabeth R. Baer, *The Golem Redux: From Prague to Post-Holocaust Fiction*

Eileen M. Hunt, *Artificial Life After Frankenstein*

Yxta Maya Murray, *The World Doesn't Work That Way, but It Could*

Sara Agnes Rice Pryor, *Reminiscences of Peace and War*

Tomás Rivera, *. . . y no se lo tragó la tierra / . . . And the Earth Did Not Devour Him*

León Salvatierra, *To the North / Al norte*

Mary Wollstonecraft Shelley, *Frankenstein; or, The Modern Prometheus*

Luis Alberto Urrea, author of *Good Night, Irene* and many other renowned novels, is referenced without a specific book title.

Book Club Questions

1. What are some of the similarities between *Chicano Frankenstein* and the Mary Shelley classic? What are some of the differences?

2. Discuss the impact of the news briefs and interviews. What do these faux-factual documents add to the story? What is your impression of the president of this alternate United States?

3. How would the man's experience be different if his physical characteristics didn't mark him as a reanimated person? Have you ever been judged based on your appearance? The man meets people who pretend to be allies but really aren't, like his coworker Norman. Have you ever worked with someone who put on a show of liking you? How did that affect your time at that job? How does Norman contrast to Tina, the colleague who gives the man helpful dating advice?

4. There are multiple scenes where the man goes out running at night. How do you interpret those? What do these solo moments add to your understanding of the character?

5. Other modern *Frankenstein* retellings include *The Strange Case of the Alchemist's Daughter* by Theodora Goss, *Pride and Prometheus* by John Kessel, *Frankenstein in Baghdad* by Ahmed Saadawi, *Spare and Found Parts* by Sarah Maria Griffin, and *Unwieldy Creatures* by Addie Tsai. Have you read any of them? Which of the titles alert the reader that they are connected to the Shelley tale

and which ones don't? Why do you think Daniel Olivas chose *Chicano Frankenstein* as the title of his novel?

6. When they are at the museum, Faustina says: "Look at *The Walking Man*. Would you change it if you could?" Consider Faustina's statement. How does her question relate to her growing feelings for the man?

7. Dr. Prietto says he doesn't want to be a "superfluous man." What does he mean by that? Do you agree with his decision to share clues to the past with the people he reanimated?

8. Reanimated subjects, Dr. Prietto reveals, are known to be honest. How do you see this character trait showing up in the man?

9. *Chicano Frankenstein* is full of Pasadena landmarks. Name a few of them. Why do you think the author chose to include specific businesses? Does having a concrete, real-world setting help anchor the plot?

10. Did the pill shortage add tension to your understanding of the man's life expectancy? Why do you think the author included pharmaceutical companies as part of the novel?

11. Why do you think the author chose not to give the man a name? How did it affect your understanding of his character?

12. Did your impression of the relationship between Faustina and the man change over the course of the novel? If so, how?

FOREST
AVENUE
PRESS